Beauty's Story

Rita Ese Edah

Beauty's Story

First published in 2014 by

Panoma Press

48 St Vincent Drive, St Albans, Herts, AL1 5SJ, UK

info@panomapress.com

www.panomapress.com

Book layout by Charlotte Mouncey

Printed on acid-free paper from managed forests.

ISBN 978-1-909623-55-2

To my children:
Eguolo, Aghogho and Ufuoma.
Thanks for giving me three reasons to carry on…

And also to my mum, Sussy,
and to the memory of my Mummy Phyllis.

PROLOGUE

23ʳᵈ June 2006
Beauty

I was scratching myself for I'd begun to itch all over… it was all I could do to get my thoughts in order.

"And you never thought to tell me this before?"

"I'm sorry, okay," Theo began.

"And so should you be, you lying conniving back-stabbing bastard!"

With each word, I'd flung an item at him. He ran round the kitchen playing 'dodge crockery', and then I went after him with two of the largest white dishes screaming, "Get out, get out of my life, now, get out…"

"Beauty, I'm sorry, we can work this out."

The more he said that, the angrier – and louder – I got. Then he stopped running and turned to face me. "Now put those dishes down or else…"

"Or else what? You'll call the police? You are the police, so arrest me, you bastard."

"Beauty! Stop it!"

Now he was holding my arms. I was screaming, "Leave me alone," as I wriggled, trying – and failing – to free myself from his grip.

He was shaking me. "Stop it! Stop it, let's talk this through." He was shaking me. Vigorously. Whipping my head back and forth; he kept shaking me, even as my screams gradually petered into a whimper…

CHAPTER 1

New Year's Eve 2000 (31st December 1999)
Beauty

I know the every imperfection of my face: the skin that is too tight, too dry, too pinched and too sallow; the lines that have suddenly appeared around the eyes – eyes that are too cloudy to be brown, that display some form of dirty, gritty grey-green. These eyes are so quick to mist, even now, as I attempt to apply some make-up to cover up the material facts, so that I can appear normal at Mel's.

I really wanted to be home this New Year's Eve. We're on the brink of a new millennium and I want to be home. Or at least with Theo. But like all hardworking police officers, he's had to go to work. Not only are they concerned about the usual drunken fracas that tends to attend New Year's Eves' gatherings, there seems to have been some increased anxiety over something or other, which of course Theo will not share with me – after all, he doesn't want me to bother my pretty little head over his work issues (his words, not mine). I'd read in the press about the hijackings in Kathmandu and the fears about terrorists and end-of-the-world cultists. But no, we don't discuss such matters…

So anyway, he's gone off to work. I'd considered joining the Thameside party parade, but of course Theo objected. So I'd resolved to eat and sleep myself into the New Year until Mel barged in. It was at times like this that I regret the key-sharing deal we struck a few years ago.

"Why are you still in bed at this time of day? And

why are you not picking up the phone?"

I come back from a baby-chasing dream to see Mel glowering, arms akimbo, frowning her questions at me. I'd given birth to the first baby of the millennium in an ambulance, but she sprouted wings and attempted to fly away as I held desperately to her ankle... aarrgghh!!!

"Good morning to you too," I managed.

"That's not good enough, Beauty, it's not morning, it's way past 2pm and I've been trying to reach you all day."

Pulling myself into a sitting position, I shrugged, "Well, it was you who taught me that morning starts when you wake up, right? So it's my morning, whatever the time might be."

"Okay, if you insist. I'm glad to see your humour returning – you had me worried though. I know you haven't been the same since..."

"Don't. Please. I'm fine. Really."

I see her bite her lips. But... I don't want to talk about it. At least not with Mel. It's enough that I have to dream about them almost every time I get a shut-eye. I want to talk with Theo. But he's hardly home. Even when he is...

Anyway, so that's when I fall in line with Mel's plan to see in the New Year at hers, along with her Joshua and Ashleigh. "Daisy and Rob will be there also," she threw in almost as an afterthought. At least there'd be no strangers tonight, she promised, and it's good to spend this evening with family and friends.

"I totally agree. But Theo won't be there," I pouted.

"Theo is doing what he has to do, Beauty, and you know that."

"Yes, I do," I nodded, thinking I might as well 'grow up'.

"Then act like you do. See you later then?"

"Sure, Sis. I'll see ya!"

With a hug and a kiss, she was gone like a breeze.

So here I am. I've been trying to get ready in the past hour or so. I'm really not in the mood… but I should at least appear presentable. Which is difficult if your eyes betray you at the drop of a hat, every now and then. Which is difficult if your hair has a mind of its own and the kinks just seem to get more stubborn when you can least afford the time or the humour. Which is difficult when you can't find what to wear because of the rapid and frequent change in your body composition, because you can't decide what suits you and what doesn't, and because your master cheerleader is not around to give you a second opinion. And because you now hate to shop.

Eventually I decide on a pastel, tie-dye, silky, layered, green skirt with a matching blouse. The elasticated waist covers a multitude of sins, as does the smocked bodice top that could be mistaken for a maternity blouse. The hem of the skirt is just shy of my ankles, the only part of my anatomy along with my wrists that don't seem to alter in size. Taking a step back for an overall view, I decide that I am content.

My silver Mary Janes with a matching handbag, chunky fashion beads and a pair of small hoops complete the façade. I choose to carry these in my day bag and walk to Mel's in my comfy boots.

Deciding on a top coat was usually easy. But not tonight. My favourite ones were bought by Theo. If he won't be with me, then I won't take a piece of him along. I opt for my faithful black ski jacket.

The 15 minutes to Mel's should lift my spirit. She is right. I could do with getting out of the house more… this may be the beginning of a New Year's resolution. I whisper a "thanks, Mel", pick up my bag and, on the spur of the moment, decide to take out my mobile phone, leaving it behind on the coffee table.

New Year's Eve 2000 (31st December 1999)
Melody

I look forward to the day when I can move into a house, with spacious rooms, with at least two receptions and a kitchen that can actually hold all my white goods and myself, Joshua and Ashleigh at one and the same time. And a garden – oh to be able to host garden parties...

"What a lovely evening, Mel," Daisy cuts in with a smile, while hanging on to Rob to ensure her stagger doesn't actually result in a fall. It's the first time all evening I've seen her without the swirling red in her goblet. This time she has a variety of bites on her plate. She says she finds the *chinchin* incredible and the *puff-puffs* absolutely divine. I'm glad I threw these Nigerian delicacies into the mix of mini quiches, sausage rolls, salmon fritters and buffalo wings. The carrot and celery sticks made a good contrast in taste and colour – and so far, that seems to be the main purpose they have served, just like the accompanying hummus.

"I'm glad you're having a good time, darling, only a couple of hours to go now."

"Certainly. And this is the only time in my life that I'll welcome in a new millennium. Thank you so much for making it such a special evening."

"Oh don't fuss, Daisy, the pleasure really is all mine."

And it was. If they hadn't come round, I'd have been stuck in this flat with the kids – not that I'd never left them home alone before, but would certainly not have wanted to do that on a night like this. I'd have had no adult to banter with as has been the bane of my existence for ages now. I'd have had too much time to think about all that is wrong in my life and I'd have either drunk or cried myself to sleep and missed out on a real, positive experience. And Rob and Daisy are a pleasure to watch, a picture of all that can be right in a relationship. Just like Beauty and Theo, except that because of Theo's line of work, it's difficult to get him into social settings like this, and it's hard for Beauty sometimes. Today, for example.

I'm glad she's here though. But I've been so busy entertaining that we haven't had a chance for a sisterly chat. Now might be the time because since everyone seems satisfied with eats, drinks and dancing, it's winding down a bit. Josh and Ash are in my bedroom on the PlayStation; Daisy and Rob are huddled on one of the two-seater sofas and Beauty and I on the other. The TV is screening parties from across the world but mostly focusing on our own Trafalgar Square and the Millennium Dome.

"So! How did you come up with a New Year party idea at such short notice?" Beauty brings me back from the scenes of jollity.

"When I woke up this morning to the recollection of my last half-hour at work last night, I knew if I didn't do something quickly, the rest of the year and the beginning of the next would be pretty miserable."

"Really? Tell me, what happened?"

"I don't know that I should – it will be like pouring

water over a nice little fire."

And it would have been. Just the thought of it even… the pushy bosses, the heaving shop floor, the winding queues and the fretful fitful customers. And the one who said to his spoilt little girl – five or six at the most – "If you don't behave yourself and be a good girl, in 10 years' time you'll be out of my house and you'll end up as a checkout girl. And then, you tell me how many Barbie dolls you think you can buy then!"

Beauty was nudging me. "Hey! Wakey wakey! Where did you go just then?"

"Work," I mutter. "I beg your pardon, I'm back now."

With a smile I pick up my wine glass, swirl it around before taking a sip and recalling how the rest of my time there was spent serving with a plastic smile frozen on my face. I tip my raised glass towards Beauty and say, "Well, you know, the customer is always right," and down the rest of its contents.

"Anyhow, I'm glad you're here. And you're well. I've got a lot to be thankful for. Josh and Ash, they get on so well together, they are doing so very well, they make me feel several inches taller. In another hour, we'll be in another year, another millennium… may all our dreams come true."

"Hear, hear! May all our dreams come true!" Rob echoes.

"And what are your dreams for the New Year, Rob?"

It's really good to see Beauty reaching out again. Rob beams our way, hugging Daisy even tighter, her little red head bobbing in delight. "We are hoping that the year 2000 is the one that sees us as parents – by this time next year, may we be gathered together with one or even two little ones in our midst."

"Let's drink to that," Beauty announces, passing round the wine.

By now the children are back in the living room, with red grape Schloer in their wine glasses, everyone chattering and watching as one by one the nations of the world burst into the new millennium – the Eiffel Tower display was spectacular by the way – and the countdown begins with Big Ben. As the last second is counted in and we join the screaming revellers – friends and strangers hugging one another in Trafalgar Square to the backdrop of the most extraordinary fireworks display I ever saw – I cannot help noticing Beauty wipe away a tear. And I think I know why. Theophilus Babafolue.

New Year's Eve 2000 (31st December 1999)
Theo

There is something about this night that is different from every other New Year's Eve. And I'm sure it's much more than the fact of an approaching new millennium. It's almost as if a whole new world were boding. Impending. Threatening, even. Would it have to do with the heightened concern expressed during the *Operation Dolphinoes* brief last week, repeated again this morning?

It's been a quiet evening – quiet in the sense that there's been no major incident. Simon and I have strolled around the precincts of the Greenwich Peninsula and all we could see were people. Normal, regular, happy, some drunk and over merry, but regular ordinary people. Her

Majesty is to open the Dome later tonight so I cannot afford to allow my senses to lull – which can happen with too much introspection.

Tony Blair has already set the Millennium Wheel rolling when he fired a laser beam across the Thames a few minutes ago. A pity the wheel has to roll empty while over 200 guests are bound to be downcast at having had the ride of a lifetime cancelled at the 11th hour. However, safety first. Always.

"It all feels normal to me, Simon, what do you think?"

"Was thinking the same, mate. Yet, in a few minutes, it will be a new year, a new century, a new world."

"Which we still have to keep safe. For Queen and Country."

"For Queen and Country," Simon echoes before we knock knuckles, an act which seemed to lighten my steps.

We walk briskly towards the Greenwich Observatory. I want to be able to call Beauty as soon as possible after midnight. I know she's not too happy when I do long shifts especially on important days like this. But this comes with the territory. Especially on a night such as this. She knows that. And she agrees that it has much better prospects than the traffic warden by day and security guard by night life I was leading some seven years ago. So yes, she understands. And she'll be fine…

And I feel better that she's safe and warm at home, not wobbling along in the midst of drunken revellers down the Thames in the name of celebrating the new millennium with spectacular walls of flames. And I'm glad I was despatched to the cordoned-off part of Greenwich. We've only had to encourage a few disgruntled restaurateurs whose grouse is that business is slower than your average

Friday night. I smile at the recollections of our little chit-chat: "Safety, my friends, safety first, always."

Now that the official celebrations are over – Her Majesty's on her way to Balmoral and the Blairs are back at Number 10 – it's time to call Beauty...

The millennium bug didn't bugger my phone – or did it? I'm surprised that she hasn't called – not one missed call from Beauty, and not one text, yet I've got loads from so many others including Mel. Oh well, I'll call her before responding to any of the others...

She is such a light sleeper, why isn't she picking up? And no, I don't want to leave a voicemail, not on the mobile, and certainly not on the landline. I'm sure she's okay, or else Mel would have said something...

It isn't till I get home and find her phone on the coffee table and see the well-dressed bed that I panic...

CHAPTER 2

March 2001
Beauty

I wish I didn't have to look in the mirror, every morning, every night. For I know the every imperfection of my face. The nose that is a veritable 'oxygen consumer'. I used to laugh when they'd called me that at school. I was never going to give them the satisfaction of knowing how much it hurt. At 12, I was already aware that my nose was largely disproportionate to the rest of my body. I didn't need anyone to rub it in. But they did. And it stung. And even though Aunty Mary said I was still growing and that my whole body would catch up and line up nicely, I don't believe it ever did. And well, it's too late now.

And what about these laughter lines that were hardly brought on by laughter? And the double chin that disappears every once in a while only to pop back again with a vengeance? Who was it that invented mirrors?

Getting ready for work – getting ready to leave the house for any reason – is always an uphill task. Yet, after stepping out I do feel better, especially when I'm attending to others, or lost in their world. Working in the library is just super as far as I'm concerned. In the midst of books. And people. And books. Okay, with computers and stuff now, but still, finding out information, giving out information... no time to stand before a cold, impersonal and impartial judge to take stock of my imperfections.

Here, at work, I can hide from myself.

Well, could. Because for some time now, especially since I've been made head of the Children's Library, I'm finding it more and more difficult to leave my broodiness at home. I'm forever faced with children, from wee babies to pre-schoolers, organising their stay and play, board game times, story times and more. Sometimes, out of nowhere, I just feel a tightening in my tummy; other times, a bloatedness and, more recently, a filling up of my breasts and a tingling of my nipples.

These strange manifestations first happened at last year's New Year's Eve party when Rob announced their desire to start trying for a baby. All of a sudden I felt as though I was going to be sick and my tummy tumbled in waves of slush. But for the glass of wine, I don't know what would have happened.

Maybe nothing. As nothing has happened since Frankie. Theo says it's for lack of trying. Mel says my body needs to rest anyway. And I say – nothing. I don't even feel up to seeing my GP just yet…

I step out and head for my lunch meeting with Daisy – I love Wednesdays.

She's already at our *Renee's* rendezvous, uncharacteristically early, her mug looking like it needs refilling, her face all flushed. She lights up my world with her cutest smile, but I can see that her eyes aren't smiling.

"What's up, baby girl?" Although she's only about a couple of months younger than me, I see Daisy as my 'baby sister' and Mel's 'baby'. Her parents are both Mel's godparents and mine, and her grandparents used to be neighbours of my maternal grandparents – the white wing of my family tree. Both our families have shared many happy and sad moments through the years.

"Chiquitita, tell me what's wrong," I intone.

She chuckles, "Now I know why you weren't called Harmony."

"Okay, Andrew Lloyd Webber, you're not getting off that easily. Really, what's up?"

"Beauty, I had my period this morning."

"Oh."

"Exactly."

We order our usuals from the *All Day Breakfast* section. They make the greatest scrambled eggs ever, *Renee's*, what with cream, butter and a pinch of black pepper added to the mix before it's cooked, not afterwards, on the hob. And certainly not the reheated from frozen gunge that I had the misfortune of eating at one of the so-called top restaurants in the city. Since that experience, I always ask how it's made before I order scrambled eggs.

"So tell me, Daisy, what exactly is going on?"

Trying to steady her voice, she says, "Nothing. Precisely nothing. That's the problem."

She goes on to tell me all about how they'd decided to leave starting a family until they'd established the business. Now that was on an even keel, Rob was running it nicely. And although she was still full time for now, she would scale back her hours over time to accommodate her needs and the baby's.

"Everything has gone according to plan, so I am not unduly stressed."

"Apart from the stress of waiting to get pregnant?"

"Precisely."

"What can I say? You know my story... don't give up hope, and try and relax... that's what I've been told, and that's all I can give to you... keep hoping..."

As we disengage from the firm hug, I notice the anguish has drained from her face.

"How's Rob?"

"You know, Beauty, but for him, I'd be lost. Period. He rolls with my every mood and tumbles with my every scrape. I am so grateful for him, don't know what I would do or be without him – such a wonderful man…"

I silently agree with Daisy. She is lucky in Rob.

"Here I am carrying on about myself. What about you, how are you bearing up?"

"Honestly, I don't know that I am. Since the last time, I haven't even missed a period again… and sometimes I wonder if I ever will."

And I was surprised to hear myself say this out loud to another living soul…

March 2001
Melody

I don't know why people complain about Mondays. If I could opt to take any two days off, it would be Wednesday and Saturday. If there was any day when I would curse myself for getting off track on my *Access to Medicine* course, it would be a Saturday. If there was any day when I would curse Nick for luring me off my planned course of action and then bleeding me dry and leaving me on the kerb, it would be a Wednesday. These are days to phone in sick – terrible days to get out of bed – I could scratch them from my calendar and just sleep through. These were the days when my singing in the shower was more like a dirge.

It was only meant to have been temporary. Finding my feet, it was the first proper job I had with a contract and everything. The part-time flexible pay-as-you-go hours were good for me then. I have sometimes built up to 40 hours a week with the optional overtime. After all these years though, I am still just a checkout girl.

Yes, I've been employee of the month once – that was when I'd threatened to go to the employment tribunal with indecent assault charges against the night supervisor. I was pleased at the time that management took my complaint seriously, ensured Mr Lust disappeared and my payoff was a plaque displayed in the shop for the whole of that month. I've often wondered what would have happened if I'd pursued the matter further. Would I have received a handsome compensation package? Would that have motivated me to have followed another course in my life? Maybe. Maybe not. I still had the children to think about. And I'm glad I did. Think about them, that is.

They've turned out okay, more than okay. They get on very well together. Do their chores, homework and are pretty much self-sufficient. There's nothing like Joshua and Ashleigh Iroro to bring the sunlight back into my life.

My heart aches for Beauty – three miscarriages in six years and then nothing. And for Daisy whose light seems to be going out. I should pray more. I should go to church more. Oh God! Please forgive me for only thinking about you when I need something. At least this time it's because of other people – Amen.

While we are on the subject – can you please send me somebody who would stay, who would want to spend the rest of their life with me, who would want to share mine?

Do I have to always be the spare wheel at social functions? I'm tired of being paired up with strangers – am I really that bad that nobody wants to be with me? Not that I blame anyone – even I don't always want to be with myself.

What will I do when the children grow up and leave home? What will I do when my fingers get curled up from arthritis and I can't scan items at the till anymore? Will I end my days cooking meals for one? Or worse still, re-heating ready-to-eat meals for one? What if I suffer from osteoporosis and I sustain a fall? What if I die in my sleep, how long will I lie rotting away before somebody notices?

Oh dear. This is depressing. And I'm not at work yet. How am I going to survive this day? I know – I flick open my mobile phone and make straight for the gallery full of snapshots of Ash's first day at ballet class… Josh's first fencing match… more recent photos at Ash's 11th birthday last August and Josh's 13th in September. I am smiling and weeping at the same time – who said teenagers had to be monsters? If only Nick could see him now… if only he'd stayed…

I resolved, once again, that it doesn't matter about my mistakes of yesterday or my fears for tomorrow. Today I have the best children in the world. And I will allow my heart to be glad.

March 2001
Ashleigh (aged 11)

School today is just pants.
I was so looking forward to starting secondary school

last September. I'd once again be in the same school as Josh; I'd bin my jumper and put on blazers, blouses and blue miniskirts (that are meant to be knee length – Mum mustn't find out!).

St Katherine's High! I got into St Katherine's High!

What a waste of time.

I remember my first day just like yesterday. Tuesday 5th September 2000. Mum had ironed my blouse. My pleated skirt and navy blazer were hanging proudly on the door of my box-bedroom. My black Clarks were smiling at me on the floor and my Nike backpack was simply telling me to 'Just do it'! It's a slightly longer walk than to my primary school, but hey, who cares? I'd be walking to school once again with Josh.

I would walk to the ends of the earth with Josh.

Mum sees us to the door, then goes back inside to get ready for work. Josh and I race down the five flights of stairs, so happy we aren't too high up the tower block because those lifts always stank of wee. And Monday mornings there's usually vomit mixed in as well.

We turn left off St Katherine's Court, go past St Katherine's Point and then right on to St Katherine's Road, as if going towards Stratford.

Soon we are rounding the corner from the newsagent's. Then Josh slows and whispers, "Ash, I'm going to have to make a dash for it."

"Hunh?"

"I'm sorry, but I can't walk into school with you."

"Because…?" I'm cocking my ear, stifling a giggle.

"I can't tell you just now, but I swear, one day you'll understand."

And he shoots off. Just like that.

I can't remember the rest of the day except that I managed to fight back the tears – no use introducing myself as 'cry baby'. I faintly remember some of the other children on purpose brushing past me on the way to the dining hall for lunch. That's about it really. No biggie. The only disaster was being in the same school as Josh and not knowing it.

Anyway, I'm used to the routine now. We leave the flat together, chat and carry on until we get near the newsagent's, then Josh makes a dash for it.

Today, though, I really wish he would walk with me into school. It is my class recitation event at whole school assembly. Every week since October, a class from each year group has taken the assembly. They each came up with different bits for the show. Today is class 7D's turn. We (actually, 'they' – I just went along with it) had decided on a recitation marathon. Each of us is to come up with a story, song, poem, monologue, a drama piece, a work of art or something that had to do with *uncertainty*. Although each person was to do it alone, if it was a piece of dialogue, then two or three could do it together. They could even sing a duet if they wanted. All they needed to do was sell it to Mr Baker, our form tutor.

I knew that nobody would want to work with me. And I didn't really want to work with anyone – except Josh, who is not in my class anyway and wouldn't walk with me to school. So I didn't bother with the drama. I just went to Aunty Beauty at the library and she helped me come up with something.

So. Here we are today. The day. I've re-read the piece to myself like a hundred times now and practised speaking it out in front of the mirror, just like Aunty Beauty said:

To be, or not to be: that is the question:
Whether 'tis nobler in the mind to suffer
The slings and arrows of outrageous fortune,
Or to take arms against a sea of troubles,
And by opposing end them? To die: to sleep;
No more; and by a sleep to say we end
The heart-ache and the thousand natural shocks
That flesh is heir to, 'tis a consummation
Devoutly to be wish'd. To die, to sleep;
To sleep: perchance to dream: ay, there's the rub;
For in that sleep of death what dreams may come
When we have shuffled off this mortal coil,
Must give us pause: there's the respect
That makes calamity of so long life...

I'm glad Aunty Beauty encouraged me not to do the whole thing, because now I'm really scared. Even though I can say it in my sleep.

Mum's still in bed having had a late night shift. Josh's had his Weetabix and is waiting for me, trying to be patient. Whistling. Tapping his foot. He wouldn't leave without me but would whine if we left later than 7.35 as it would mean he had to run faster and further to catch up with his friends. Why he needs me for cover, heaven only knows. Mum completely trusts him. She practically handed over my upbringing to him.

Pass the parcel is my best party game. Dad passes me to Mum. Mum passes me to Josh. And Josh passes me to... myself. Pretty neat eh? Now that would have been a better monologue to recite today. I would not have been afraid of forgetting my lines.

Because. This is my life: Eleven. Alone. Unknown.

CHAPTER 3

April 2001
Beauty

I remember the first time he called me 'useless'. At least, the first time when it didn't come across as a joke. That's when I should have left him... But – probably he was right. Just maybe he was. For here I am, sitting, paralysed on the sofa, having received news that my dad's in hospital. With a stroke.

I was pregnant with Alex then. We agreed to not ask the sex so as to be genuinely surprised on arrival day. We'd just moved from the crummy little rented flat to a three-bed terraced house on St Martin's Lane, not too far from Green Street. Theo had recently completed his training and was busy settling into work. So the task of buying furniture for the home fell on my shoulders. I didn't mind really – I could shop for England.

Of course, as we needed to be careful with money, a lot of the big ticket items – especially impersonal ones – we were going to buy second-hand. I had window-shopped for so many as I either walked to work or to Mel's so that when the time was right, I knew which electronic shop to go to, to pick our maiden TV set from – well, it got delivered actually. After they'd come, set it up and gone, I sat staring at the box from a combination of fatigue and excitement, looking forward to Theo's return.

He wasn't pleased. I could tell from the way his jaws set, his fingers clenched and his eyes slit as he flicked the remote control from one channel to another, that he was seething. But I couldn't tell why. Unable to draw him out, I concluded that it must have something to do with work, and he'd share it in his own time. Aunty Mary's words sprang to me as if on cue, "The way to a man's heart is his stomach."

Pulling myself together, I went about making dinner for us – well, really more for him as it was his favourite: *pounded yam* with *egusi* soup. The soup was already portioned in the freezer so all I had to do with that was reheat it in the microwave. He had complained about this previously but he's come to accept that cooking traditional soups from scratch on a daily basis was a pipe dream in which I wasn't going to indulge.

The *pounded yam,* however, is a different story entirely. It's hit and miss for me, getting the consistency right, but I've been lucky these past few months that it's come out firm but not hard, and almost always completely lump-free. Tonight, it had just a few very tiny lumps scattered here and there. He's had it that way before so I was quite surprised when he scraped back his chair from the table and stomped to the sink to wash his hands.

"What's the matter, love?"

"What's not the matter? How useless can you be?" He punctuated each syllable with a bang on the work surface.

"I beg your pardon?"

"Look, I work hard all day. Come home to a TV that has no Teletext."

"Of course it has Teletext – it said so in the shop."

"Well, I've checked it inside and out – it has no Teletext and that is one function that is important to me in a television set. My wife, an educated woman, a librarian for that matter, could not manage to get that right."

Speechless, I rummaged through my handbag to find the ticket that had the list of features which had earlier advertised the colour television set. Staring at me in black and white was my error. It listed *FST* which I must have read as *TXT*. He was right. I missed it.

"I'm sorry, love, it was an error."

"Of course you'll say so. What I just don't understand is how stupid you can be sometimes."

"Theo, I said I was sorry. It could have happened to anyone, no need to make it personal."

"I'm not making it personal, just pointing out the facts. Intelligence is not common sense, and you are obviously lacking in that department. Can't buy a TV right, can't make a meal right. Good-for-nothing useless woman…"

By this time I was upstairs, in bed, and of course, in a flood of tears. But the ranting continued. How Mel could make *pounded yam*, after all, she was half-caste like me, so why couldn't I? How Daisy managed the finances and purchases in their home, and she'd have known what TV to buy. Why didn't such wisdom rub off on me? Stupid and useless, that's why. *Born throw-way* spoilt brat… and on and on he went…

I couldn't contain the sobs that wracked my bosom as I wailed into the pillow which I held against my face. Eventually, as if from a distance, I heard the slamming, and soon enough, the screeching of the tyres. And then the silence. But I couldn't stop the weeping, not even in my fitful sleep.

I awoke on Sunday near noon needing to use the loo. As I stirred, I felt wet and I winced – when did I last bed wet? This couldn't be happening again! What will Theo say? I flew to the bathroom only to find I was bleeding. Unable to reach Theo, I got the ambulance which raced me to Newham General. Too late.

Alex was my second bereavement that I am aware of. Charlie was the first. (And I can't stop crying now.) Mum died due to complications following my birth. I never met her. Now Dad is sick in hospital. And there is nothing I can do. And, not for the first time in my life, I feel completely, utterly useless.

Dad was gutted at Mum's death. He cut short his studies at King's College London. He was a third-year medical student. He allowed Nan and Grandpa to look after us all in Hackney for three months while he sorted travel documents for Mel and me. I had my first solids from the hands of my Aunty Mary.

And now he lies in hospital because of a stroke. And I don't know what to do. And the tears won't stop rolling down my polka-dotted olive cheeks.

April 2001
Melody

My children cannot see me fall apart. I did that once and it nearly cost me both of them. Looking back, it wasn't because Nick had disappeared (though that didn't help). I think it's because Ash was such an image of Beauty at her birth that I couldn't stand to hold her without cringing on the inside. She took me right back to when Beauty was born.

Mum lost a lot of blood. The medics didn't realise early enough that Beauty was presenting breech. By the time they did, they reckoned it would be faster and safer to continue with the natural birth. Two hours later, Beauty had torn her way out… Mum was apparently too exhausted to fight, and Dad's light went out with her.

All of a sudden, I was not only technically orphaned at age five, I'd also become a mother. And for a long time, I couldn't hold my baby sister, even though for the past few months I'd been looking forward to her arrival. I couldn't look into Beauty's beautiful lake-like eyes without wanting to scratch them out. And everyone said how beautiful she looked (and she was cute) and how lucky Dad and I were to have her. And they asked me to be a big girl. But I didn't want to be a big girl. I wanted my mummy and my daddy. I wanted all I had before Beauty came and took them away from me. And I wanted to hurt her as she had hurt me. Sometimes, when no one was looking, I would pinch her ear lobe or pull a strand of her curly chestnut hair. She was naturally a crier anyway so no one suspected anything. They just fussed over her which annoyed me even more…

I thought I had outgrown all of that. But when Ash turned up with her feisty little balled-up fists and powerful diaphragm that belted her displeasures – which seemed to be many – it all came crashing around me again. This was Beauty all over again, and I couldn't handle it. I was convinced she was sent to punish me for what I did to Beauty as a baby (though I never told anyone this), and I was scared that I might hurt my baby in some way.

And so it was that I couldn't bear to touch Ash. Beauty mothered her (and Josh) for those first few dark months. I couldn't stop weeping. My milk production apparatus wouldn't stop churning, yet this nightmare of a child wouldn't suckle, wouldn't stop hollering… a lot of that period is still very hazy. But I recall the paralysis that alternated with deep gut pain… the same as I feel now after speaking with Aunty Mary on the phone.

I cannot afford to lose my daddy. Not just yet anyway. We've got to find a way to have him moved into a private hospital. We've got to actually act on the plan to go home for a holiday one year – this summer has to be it, and I want Josh and Ash to see my dad on his feet, not gowned in a hospital bed – and certainly not in a box.

I will not cry.

I must get rid of the shakes before the children return.

Better still, I should go and see Beauty.

I opt to take the back roads – I don't really feel like smiling at anyone. I've got to find a way to see that Dad survives this. How I wish I'd pursued my dream of studying medicine. Maybe if he hadn't given up his studies, he'd have been in a better position to have prevented this. What causes a stroke anyway? Could it have been avoided? How soon can he be cured? Can he be healed? Aunty Mary says he can't speak on the phone right now. I've got to hear his voice again. That voice that used to sing my name, that used to soothe me to sleep, that used to duet with mine… I want my dad back. I want my daddy.

My head is spinning and the tears flowing freely by the time I slump beside Beauty on her sofa. For the first time ever, we cry in unison through our cuddle.

When it eventually subsides, I hold Beauty at arm's length, looking into her watery splotchy eyes. I say, "Forgive me, Sis. I have a confession to make."

I don't know what she expected but a flicker of fear flittered through her face. I hold her closer. "I'm really sorry, I used to hate you."

Her relief was tangible. "Is that all?" she sighed.

"Seriously."

"Well, you were mean to me sometimes – I don't think I've recovered from your feeding my feather boa to the vacuum cleaner – but then you were always protective of me, terrorising all potential bullies… and I've always admired you… thank you."

I choke up again. "See how gracious you are. But I blamed you in my heart for Mum's death. And to me, Dad died with her – he was never again the father I used to know… and now he's laid up in hospital and we are thousands of miles away…"

After the next wave of waterworks, it was Beauty who disengaged first. "So tell me, big sister, when did you stop hating me?" Her eyes held no reproach, just curiosity.

So I told her.

It was when she planted the seed of the idea for us to run away from home in Warri and return to Nan in the UK. I was 18, and Beauty nearly 13. It took us about a year to carry it out, but that was the best year of my life as it was. We were to lose Nan a few months later – she never recovered from Grandpa's passing, but we were not to know that at the time.

I was about five when we went to Warri. Beauty was a baby. Aunty Mary took us under her large warm wings and devoted herself to our welfare, nursing Dad back to health. A couple of years later he'd got married and within five years Rosa (whom I hated calling Mum but was smacked if I didn't) had given him three girls. I was pleased to have been shipped off to an all girls' boarding school for my secondary education.

This was where I really began to realise how much I'd lost, how different I was and how adrift. I was grateful, however, that Beauty didn't come to join me there. She couldn't bear the thought of being away from home, and Dad, of course, obliged her.

While at school, I recall girls telling of their various experiences of circumcision. For the most part, even though it was the done deal, many were not told until they were taken to the venue. And yes, they were fussed over afterwards and showered with new clothes and food, celebrating their welcome into adulthood, yet it held no appeal for me. And as I grew older, my dread of being tricked into being mutilated took on a life of its own. During one Christmas, I thought I needed to talk to Dad about this and get his assurance that Beauty and I would be exempt from this practice.

However, although he said he could sympathise with my position, he wouldn't guarantee that we would be spared as it was a necessary part of our culture.

Then, one day, our little orphaned cousin, Onome, who lived with us came back from a trip to the village with Rosa, extremely subdued. A few days later, lots of people came visiting, and she was elegantly dressed in traditional attire of a single English wax wrapper and matching blouse, with a light headscarf. Some of the visitors seemed to be suitors or their family members. She didn't speak much, mostly sat demurely, greeting politely and answering questions directed her way, without herself asking any. I personally took a positive dislike to all of the visitors that day – but no one was asking my opinion, not even Dad.

That night, in the girls' bedroom that we all shared, I heard Onome crying. And when she eventually fell asleep, she thrashed about, screaming, "Leave me alone, let go of my hands... my legs are hurting... you are hurting me!" When I managed to shake her awake, she looked dazed, disorientated and scared. I asked if I should get our parents, and she shook her head. I asked if she wanted to talk about her nightmare, and she shook her head. I asked if it had to do with the circumcision. She nodded. And wept... and she wouldn't let me cuddle her.

The next morning Beauty whispered to me, "If we don't get away, this will happen to us." She was right. And that was when I began to plot our exit... which ultimately resulted in another broken heart for Dad.

"But for Theo," Beauty offers quietly, "he would never have forgiven us."

We look at each other through red and swollen eyes, and know, without speaking, that we have to go home to see Dad.

May 2001
Ashleigh (aged 11)

Mum speaks on the phone a lot now to her Aunt Mary. I wish she would speak to me. She looks so sad. I wish I could help her. She tries to be strong. And when I ask what the matter is, she tries to lighten up and smile saying, "Oh it's nothing."

But it is something.

It's not to do with her work this time.

It's not to do with her boyfriends – or lack of.

It's not directly to do with money.

It's something to do with her dad.

At least she has a dad. She knows him. Can talk to her Aunt Mary about him. And to my Aunty Beauty.

I know my dad is somebody called Nick. Mum wouldn't talk to me about him. Even Josh doesn't want to talk about him. He says he doesn't want to know, and that we are better off without anyone telling us what to do.

Are we? I think somebody needs to tell Josh what to do, and that 'somebody' isn't me. He isn't listening to me. If he would, he wouldn't be skimming from Mum's purse, getting me to be a look-out on his shoplifting sprees or hanging out with them no good Sam and Jerry.

Although he still wouldn't let me walk with him into school, he has protected me from the likes of Sam and Jerry, including the girl versions – Trace and Scary Spice. So I am not bullied. Ignored largely. But that's about it. I keep to myself, and hang out with Josh when he has time for me – which is really about me doing his dirty jobs for him.

I can't snitch on him.

Mum can't see him.

Nick won't see him – or me for that matter. Actually I should have said Dad but it doesn't quite sound right.

Maybe if what I heard Mum and Aunty B discuss is true, then we are in for a big family holiday to Nigeria this summer. It would be good if it actually happens. Get to see another arm of the family. Might do Josh some good, who knows…

Would cost a bomb though… is why it hasn't happened yet…

CHAPTER 4

July 2001
Theo

We were told at Police Academy Communications Class 101 that one of the worst aspects of this job/vocation/profession/life – call it what you want – is having to tell someone that their loved one has died. The basic template we were drilled to follow was to notify the bereaved:

In person
In time
In plain language
In pairs
With compassion

What they did not tell us was that the hardest and worst part ever was having to tell your own loved one that their loved one has died. And although this template was inadequate, it's all I have to work with. Having said that, Aunty Mary's words also rang in my ears: "You are not merely an in-law, but also our son. Please be careful how you tell them. Please look after them for me."

I'd promised her I would. That was two days ago. I've critically examined my options. If I told them separately, it made it more personal and each person would have the space to deal with it in their own way before coming together. However, that way, there was the risk of the one blurting it out inadvertently to the other which could be devastating. There was also the little problem of deciding which of them to inform first.

Telling them together would mean they each heard it first-hand from me. At the same time…

But, how do I go about showing compassion to my wife and to her sister at the same time?

Washing the car was such a good stress buster. As was the vacuuming. And the mopping. And taking junk to the dump, and then cleaning out the inside of the car once again. Then the ironing, which I ordinarily hate with a passion…

When Beauty came back from the shops and asked what the matter was, my heart missed two beats. "What do you mean?"

"It's a Saturday, it's your day off and you're not sleeping."

"Oh. I'm not too tired."

"I can see that. What's with the marathon housework?"

"Oh that. I thought to give you a hand as Rob and Daisy are coming round later."

"They are? I thought it was just Mel?"

"Oh sorry, it must have skipped my mastermind," I chuckled.

Only, it hadn't. I arranged it with them after she'd left home.

She went ahead to reprimand me in her gentle way for being forgetful when it mattered most. Now, she said, she had to go back and get some more groceries to be sure there was enough for everyone. But there was enough for everyone – Beauty overshops as a rule – "Just in case," she would say. It was still a job to convince her though that we had enough for a simple supper for us to just enjoy some quality time with one another.

Beauty – a wiz in the kitchen even though I didn't always admit it to her – did her magic with the pasta bake. She beamed with pleasure as I grated the cheese for the topping and shredded the lettuce, diced the cucumber and sliced the tomatoes.

Sometimes I caught her eyeing me quizzically and I hoped she did not see through me into the very intents and purposes of my heart.

When the doorbell chimed at 4pm, I knew before getting it that it was Daisy and Rob. I estimated that Melody would follow in another hour or so. I wasn't wrong.

As supper drew to a close, I found I had to make frequent trips to the bathroom. At one point, Rob squeezed my shoulder. To the others, excluding Daisy, he seemed to be saying to me, "Thank you for a lovely evening." We all knew that Rob was a man of few words.

When I couldn't put it off any longer, I cleared my throat and put on my 'official voice' as I announced that I had something to say. Ensuring I made eye contact with each of them, I steeled myself on the inside as I pronounced, "Melody, Beauty, I'm sorry to inform you that your father has died."

You could have heard a pin drop.

"Aunty Mary called a couple of days ago to say he went into a coma from which he never recovered. I'm sorry."

Another long, loud silence.

"I've got to go." Melody was at the door in an instant.

"Hold on, please," Rob called after her, "let me drive you home."

"No thanks, I'd rather walk."

"That's okay, Daisy and I will walk with you."

"If you must."

After offering Beauty a hug and a kiss with their condolences, they were off. The sisters said nothing to each other.

Did I miss the 'in person' aspect?

I couldn't help admiring Melody though. She was a specimen of a woman. Strong. Independent. Almost fierce. Okay, actually fierce but in a comely way. I sometimes wish Beauty had some of her fire.

Beauty, up to 60 minutes after they'd gone, had said nothing. I didn't know whether to hold her or to leave her. So I got busy tidying away the supper things.

When she did speak it was to enquire, "When exactly did you know this?"

"On Thursday morning. Aunty Mary called me."

"And why did it take you so long to tell me?"

"I needed to get the timing right."

"I see."

She got up, went into the bedroom and shut the door behind her. I stayed out of her way for the rest of the night, wondering whether I did get the timing right.

August 2001
Melody

Staring out of the window of the Boeing 727 flight number 9571 from London Gatwick to Murtala Muhammed International Airport, Lagos, I couldn't help wondering why I've been unable to cry. Could it be because I've been very busy preparing for the trip, including having to decide whether or not to take Josh and Ash along? Josh didn't seem to mind one way or another. Ash was curious to meet the Nigerian arm of her extended family. I'd have been more inclined to spend nearly £3k on tickets home for us three if the circumstances had been different. I don't think I'll be able to forgive myself for having put it off for so long.

They both had their headphones on, tuned into whatever it was on the little screen in front of them. I'm sure I've been as absent to them these past few weeks as my dad was to me after Mum's passing. I remember being so afraid then that I might get lost in the midst of so many people at the airport. I remember needing to use the toilet and having to go in alone. When I'd finished, the door wouldn't open. Even though I called out, Daddy could not hear me because he wasn't inside the ladies with me – he was out in the lounge with Beauty. And I thought they might leave without me, and I would have to live in the toilet forever. Thinking 'forever' was a long time, I folded my woollen red coat in half, placed it on the floor in one corner of the cubicle, sat with my knees pulled up to my chin and sobbed quietly.

When eventually they knocked down the door, pulled me out and handed me to Dad who was holding a photograph of me in that same red coat, I could have kissed somebody. Instead, I stayed glued to Daddy's leg until we boarded.

Coming back to now, I consoled myself that Josh and Ash were older than I had been then, and at least they had each other for company. That always comforted me.

The heat slapped me square in the face, and I knew I was red because I was itchy. I'd forgotten to take my antihistamines. I'd been so caught up with ensuring that we had our anti-malaria tablets and yellow fever, typhoid and hepatitis vaccines that I completely forgot how unreliable my body system turned out to be in hot and strange places. Fortunately Boots the Chemist had some in stock and even though it was overpriced, I was desperate.

As we approached the Customs and Immigration clearance area, my heart sank at the length and bulkiness of the queue. Rather than move forward towards a booth in a single file, it sort of shuffled en bloc. And there were too many people leaning over the barricade in front, from where officers pointed and called people forward in no systematic way that I could decipher. From time to time the crowd parted like the Red Sea while VIPs with their hangers-on rolled past, got vaguely checked and went along their merry way.

Joshua spoke my thoughts, "How does this queue actually work?"

"In mysterious ways," Theo replied.

I'd thought it strange that he'd chosen to travel in his uniform. Now he reached into his hand luggage and took out his hat. Donning it with one hand and holding on to Beauty with the other, he said to us, "Come with me."

"Excuse me," he boomed, "excuse me," and as the crowd looked up to him in his full regalia, they made way. A couple of men met us halfway. "*Oga* sir, welcome sir, do you need anything sir?"

"Just a quick exit, I have an important meeting to attend."

"Yes sir." They now turned to the crowd and commanded, "Make way! Make way!"

All of a sudden we had two 'town criers'. Within minutes, we had cleared customs, retrieved our luggage, and got escorted to the arrivals lounge where Aunty Mary was waiting for us with Cousin Daniel who was to drive us for most of the time we were home.

Theo shook hands with our chief 'town crier' who looked into his hand then bowed from his waist down. "Thanks sir, that's very generous of you sir, have a safe journey sir, thanks sir." His companion joined in the profuse thanksgiving.

August 2001
Ashleigh (aged 11, nearly 12)

I thought it was neat that Mum decided that we went with her for her dad's funeral. It's sad and everything but we'll get to hang out together – like a normal family. What I did not know was all the stuff we had to do first.

Because Mum had been planning for us to travel this summer anyway, our passports were ready. It was cool having two nationalities because it meant we could hold two passports. Mum thought it was better than trying to get a visa. For the British passports Mum sent the forms, photos and cheque through the post. Within a few weeks, we received them through Royal Mail.

For the Nigerian passports, we had to apply in person at the Fleet Street consular office. It was quite an experience.

First of all we got lost. We took the wrong turning out of St Paul's tube station. It wasn't until about 20 minutes later that Mum asked a newsvendor who said we were going in the opposite direction to our destination. In the end we got there about an hour later than the 10am Mum had planned. She was grumpy about that. Josh was grumpy that he had to get out of bed so early in the half-term break. Me, I was just eager to see what went on in a consular office.

Not that I saw much. Just loads of people. Of all ages. And the smell – was that a combination of the sweat from so many people packed in a room without air? I'm sure some of it was baby bums that so needed wiping and air-ing. Mum said if we'd got there on time we'd have been nearer the front of the queue. So we had to be very patient. At the moment, our ticket number was 99B. They were seeing to 18A. Josh didn't want to play any games with me. He didn't want to read anything. So I left him to it and I plugged in my MP3 and browsed Mum's *Hello* magazines. I had to make it loud to drown out the noise, and hope-fully distract me from the odour. It didn't quite work that way. And it upset Mum so I had to keep turning it down, then slightly up again when she was on to something else – she kept going up to see how the queue was moving. And muttering about the inefficient system, the grizzly babies and the very loud customers.

Still, I managed to while away the time, listening to my music and daydreaming. Till about 1.30 when I need-ed to go to the loo and it turned out that they were all out of order. Mum's fuming didn't get us anywhere. In the end, we risked losing our place in the queue and went to the nearby McDonald's.

After visiting their small rooms, Mum got us lunch,

saying we might as well be set up for the rest of the day. I usually had a chicken nuggets Happy Meal. But this time, I copied Josh and asked for a Big Mac meal. And guess what? I bit into something bony, only to find out that half of my premolar had broken on my burger. Mum had to arrange a visit to the dentist for the other half to be taken out. I can tell you, that's put me off Big Macs for the rest of my life!

The rest of the afternoon just carried on as the morning. There seemed to be different people at the till, but the system was the same. Your number came up on the little screen. You took yourself and your party to the allocated window. They checked your paperwork including passport photos, then sent you to another window, where they checked that you had the right fees. And then on you went to another window for what I'm not too sure. And then you got a slip for another date if everything was in order.

Mum had all her paperwork in place including the correct amount of postal order, although she'd moaned about how inconvenient that was – they didn't accept cheque or card payments. She got another appointment to go and pick up our passports in a week's time. We didn't need to go with her on that day. Phew!

What else we needed though was jabs. If not for me, Josh would have wimped out of having them. The yellow fever one was more painful than the heps and typhoid ones. I went in first and shrugged when I came out of the nurse's room, like it was no biggie. He didn't have a choice then. And we've had to be taking those lame Larium tablets, like forever. Mum says it's much better than having to be treated for malaria fever. She sounded like she knew what she was talking about…

The Ikeja Sheraton was neat. It was the first time I'd actually stayed in a place that had air conditioning rather than radiators.

But the trip to Warri was, oh my gosh! As we drove through Lagos, we saw big yellow buses with people hanging from the doors and out of the windows. Mum said these were *molue,* the cheapest form of public transportation available in Lagos. They honked their horns all the time. Actually, all the drivers seemed to be doing was swerving and honking and yelling. Now I knew the real meaning of 'cacophony' that Mum likes to say about my music.

I think Cousin Daniel ("please call me Uncle Danny," he'd said) tried to be careful. Just as I was beginning to wonder why he didn't just drive straight on the road, I saw that he was trying to avoid potholes. He wasn't always able to do so and my backside was sore from the bouncing by the end of the seven-hour trip. Uncle Theo said it shouldn't have taken more than four. And muttered under his breath that all this roadblock nonsense still hadn't stopped.

To be honest, I'm glad he travels in his uniform because some of the police officers who stopped us looked really mean. But when they came close to the 504 station wagon and saw him in the 'owners' corner, they quickly snapped their feet together, gave a sharp salute and waved us on.

As we got off the main road on to untarred winding lanes, I guessed we must be near Granddad's home. We'd passed so many cyclists, but now they seemed like flies everywhere. I was really scared when I saw this Vespa with a woman carrying a child strapped to her back and another one between her and the cyclist who was weaving in and out of traffic. A motorcycle came between a truck and our car and he was going at such speed… looking back, what difference did ducking my head make? Duh!

Finally, we were on an unmarked road with only a few houses sprinkled here and there. When we stopped at this massive thing, I thought my mum must be from a royal family! The gates swung open after Uncle Danny spoke into the wall. Mum turned to me and Josh and said, "Welcome home, guys," and started to cry…

August 2001
Beauty

I can still see the disgust on his face, the first time he told me I wasn't a man – as if I didn't know it already, the size of my nose, my muscular arms and facial hair notwithstanding – and to quit acting like one. I retreated, the fool that I was, not intending to be macho, only wanting to air my views on something or other which right now I cannot remember.

What I cannot forget is how long it took him to tell me. To just tell me, his wife, that I'd lost my father. And when he finally did, it had to be in public. And when Mel left without a word or a hug – I could understand, she was in as much shock as I was. What I cannot understand is how he let me spend the whole night by myself. No matter how hard I try, the events of that evening keep going on like a merry-go-round in my head. Only, there is nothing merry about these rounds.

I can see how he would want to cater more for Mel's welfare than for mine.

For I am familiar with the every imperfection of my form. I'm only a couple of inches taller than the tallest dwarf. Petite, my dad, used to say. But then, he's my dad – was… Everyone else called me 'shortie', including Theo.

Mel, however, has the stature and elegance of a super-model. She could have been a Hollywood star, our Mel… and she is a super mum. She was born for stardom. When I tell her that, she just laughs. But she is a star. Always has been to me. And me, I was born to walk in her shadow. Always have. Always will. That's the bit I haven't told her yet, and don't know if I ever will.

But for her, I wouldn't have come on this trip. I wanted to visit while Dad was alive. I didn't feel up to an elaborate funeral ceremony. Plus I had nothing tangible to show for having been in England all these years. Mind you, it was good to get to meet and know the white wing of the family. Still… what have I achieved? When she saw that I wasn't budging, she got Aunty Mary on my case and she somehow convinced me that I could regret missing out on an opportunity to say goodbye to Dad, something I never had a chance to do with Mum. She insisted it would help with bringing closure. And she told me that she missed me, and wanted to see me again, irrespective of the circumstances.

So here was I, wrapped in Aunty Mary's generous bosom, sobs wracking through mine, wails pouring out of my soul that continued as though they would go on forever. Soon a whole company of women had joined me and the ululations persisted till the wee hours…

Funnily enough, I woke up the next morning feeling much lighter on the inside. The smell of *yam and pepper-soup* tickled my nostrils and the sounds of children carrying on didn't bring on a wave of nausea, an iota of longing or an ounce of anger. And for the first time since I learnt of Dad's death, I was hopeful that I could actually forgive Theo.

Two days after the interment, Theo led his family in paying the traditional homage by the son-in-law. Ordinarily, it would have been done in some three months' time but we only had 10 days altogether to spend in Warri, so the time frame had to be adjusted.

The morning opened on a bright and light note. The palm frond booths were still in place from the funeral ceremonies. Fortunately we were in proper August break so the rains had kept away, apart from the occasional showers like last night.

The women in our household had been up at the crack of dawn. After persistent nagging from Mel and me to join in the preparations, Aunt Mary's team of helpers allowed us to give a hand with the salad. Josh had been clinging to Daniel and had gone off with him on some errand or other. Ash seemed a bit lost sometimes, and followed me and Mel around like Mary's little lamb.

I hadn't seen much of my stepmum, Rosa. She'd remained mostly in her chambers. Whenever she'd come out, she was in black from head to toe. It was good to see her this morning in blue attire.

By mid-day, we were thrown out of the kitchen to go and get ready. My outfit was a white organza blouse that had white and gold appliqué. It had a square neckline with an off the shoulder short sleeve, and a discreet zipper to the side.

To be able to walk comfortably in the *up and down* lace *George* wrapper, I had to hold the bottom piece of the wrapper behind me at waist level, with my legs hip-width apart. Then I had to take the end held by my left hand across to my right side before bringing my feet together and taking the right-hand edge to the left. Aunty Mary had given me an old tie of my father's to use to secure it tightly around my waist. This bottom piece had to drop way down to my ankles. The top piece, however, I tied in a similar fashion but without the belt, and it only dropped to my calf. I could have worn it shorter or longer as I pleased.

Before going on to the *gele*, I had to ensure I'd put on my coral beaded earrings, bracelets and necklaces. I had my gold and silver open-back sandals and matching clutch purse.

The white, silver and gold *gele* was expertly knotted on my head by Aunty Mary. To the uninitiated it looked like an elaborate hat – and that is how I wore it – but it was actually a stiff 100cm by 190cm headscarf made of polyester/metallic material.

Mel and my three half-sisters would be dressed similarly, but in colours different from mine. They'd agreed on a blue motif. My coral beads were heavier and more elaborate as it was my husband and his family that were coming to pay homage.

The rising level of buzz from arriving guests created an excitement and a fear in me at one and the same time. I could hear salutations and ululations and eulogies to my late dad. I fought between the urge to cry and the wish to smile. In the end, the tears simply trickled as I recalled the way he used to say my name...

"Aunty Beauty, you look gorgeous." It was Ash, knocking and dashing into my room on the dot of four o'clock.

"So do you, my darling." She was in a maxi skirt and smart blouse, with *gele*, no doubt crafted for her by Aunty Mary.

"They want you to come now."

I took her hand and we walked into the main reception area. Mel and Josh were right behind me. My other sisters and some cousins, including Onome, followed. This entourage was then flanked on either side by a bevy of older female relations who fanned us with intricately designed handheld fans as we walked, calling out:

Iyibo 'r awveren (literally, 'Our white persons' or 'Our very important persons')

Omokiyovwin (What a beautiful child!)

Emotekoba (Daughters who are like royalty)

Ibenjamini nierhi (Benjamin had a good destiny)

We were escorted to our special booth where my dad's siblings and other family members were already seated.

Looking across to the in-laws' booth, there was Theo, resplendent in his outfit. His wrapper was a large single piece, wrapped to the left and folded casually at the top. This, however, was obscured by his shirt that fell to just above his knees. Our colours were matching in every way, except that he had a black bowler hat and a black walking stick.

Drinks and food were served as the customary introductions were made.

Then Theo's family spokesman rose. "We have come here today to give honour to an illustrious man. A simple man. A man of honesty and integrity. A kind-hearted man. One who was kind enough to allow us into his family, and bless us with his daughter. And not only that, but one who accepted our son as if he were his own. This man is our father, Benjamin Etakibuebu Iroro, who has now gone ahead of us to a better place. Today we will eat and drink and sing and dance as we remember that we have been a blessed people for having become part of Mr Iroro's family."

As if on cue, the lead singer of the live band began: "Was he a good man?"

"He was a good man," his band replied.

"Was he an honest man?"

"He was an honest man."

Family members, in-laws and guests were now joining in the response.

"Was he a handsome man?"

"He was the most handsome man of his generation!"

This carried on in various forms for a while, and then the band went into very high tempo musical numbers, and everyone was encouraged to dance with thanksgiving for the life and times of Mr Benjamin Iroro.

I surprised myself at how I tapped and swayed and moved to the African highlife rhythm. And I was surprised to see Theo join me, not only in dance, but in slapping 50 naira notes on my forehead and round my neck and arms – any bare bits of my frame. Mel and Ash did the honours of picking the money off me and off the floor while I beamed and swayed even harder. When I spread out my arms and went into the traditional rhythmic chest pops, the whole crowd went up in a wild cheer. And as I continued popping my chest, limboing downwards with intricate footwork, Theo mirrored my steps and pace, limboing opposite me and continuing to shower me with naira notes.

By the end of the evening, exhausted and exhilarated, I regained a conviction that I had long lost – that Theo, indeed, did love me.

CHAPTER 5

There's nothing like visiting Nigeria after you've been away for a while. And although it was under sad circumstances, it was a fruitful visit. Visiting with family and friends, giving a great funeral and in-laws homage to my dear father-in-law, and winning back Beauty's heart once again made it an experience worthy of the cost.

It was particularly pleasing to see my parents and family members not just being civil to Beauty and her family but giving us their full cooperation. My parents had come a long way from when I first told them I wanted to marry Beauty Iroro. I'd met Beauty and Mel one summer after the Notting Hill Carnival. I'd just completed my Political Science degree at the University of East London. I missed home dreadfully but the political climate was unsafe and Papa, a very outspoken human rights activist, had got under the skin of the military junta, so he thought it safest for me to be away from Nigeria for a while. That Christmas was the first time I'd be home in three years.

After the festivities of the season, as I began my preparations to travel back to London, my mother came up with her pet subject. "Look after yourself, my son, keep your head down, and don't wait too long to settle down and bless me with grandchildren."

That really used to irritate me. But this time, I smiled, "Your prayers might be getting answered soon."

"Really, tell me all about her." She was beaming.

And I think I was beaming too as I told her about Beauty – her grace, her patience, her intelligence, her cooking skills and the fact that we were in love with each other.

"What's her name?"

"Beauty."

"That's a lovely name. Where is she from?"

"Her father is from Warri mainland, and her mother was from London."

"Was?"

"Yes. She died soon after Beauty was born."

"How soon?"

"A few hours, I think."

"God forbid!" And she made this gesture of rolling her hand over her head and clicking her fingers at the end of the move which finishes as if writing an 'o' in the air. Her face had passed from joy to horror. Though I was deflated by her reaction, I wasn't entirely surprised, but I'd hoped it wouldn't be a major issue.

"What's wrong, Ma, I thought you'd be happy for me?"

"I was, but can't be now."

"Why not?"

"Because your father will kill me, that's one reason."

"Why so?"

She took pains to explain. That as my father was now a chief in our *Itsekiri* ethnic community, it would be disgraceful for his only son to marry from another (read as rival) ethnic group. And as if that wasn't bad enough, the bride-to-be is not even fully from that group. She's partly white. That means his grandchildren will be a mixed breed of sorts and so the chieftaincy title will not pass down my line as it must be kept pure. It didn't seem to matter that

I personally wasn't interested in the title. It didn't seem to matter either that she'd been hassling me to get married and to give her grandchildren while she still had some energy to play with them.

"There are lots of equally beautiful girls from our community that will make a fine wife for you. Why not take one of those?"

"Because I don't love anyone of those."

"If you get to know them, you will."

"How will I get to know them? I don't live here."

"The political climate is getting calmer, so hopefully you can begin to come back home more often... and of course they can visit you."

"The distance is too much for that to work."

But she insisted that it's worked in so many cases including herself and my father.

"That was a different era," I insisted, digging in my heels. "Besides, what's the other reason?"

"This is a difficult one, my son; I wish I wasn't the one to break it to you." Her pause was ominous. "A child that kills her mother is an abomination to our people and our land."

"I think you missed something here, Ma. She didn't *kill* her mother," I stressed. "She was born and her mother died soon afterwards."

"Not much difference there, is there?"

"How could she have killed her mother? She was only a baby! She was innocent."

"Her mother died at her birth. She took her mother's place."

"Do you really believe this? I thought you were now a Christian?" I felt floored by this angle.

"Yes, I am now a Christian, bless God, and I am willing to take the risk. But not everybody is ready around here. It will make the family a laughing stock, and she will be the prime suspect if any misfortune, God forbid, befalls this family, or even the wider community."

I really couldn't get my head round that. Although mentally I thought it was rubbish, still I found myself wondering whether there was any truth in it. More so, I wondered whether I was willing to risk being a pariah in my own community if I went ahead and married Beauty. Yet, it's not often you came across women who had the vital mix that was important to me – educated and with a progressive outlook to life, while being down to earth and familiar with my Nigerian cultural heritage. Being mixed race and having spent her formative years in Warri, Beauty – as well as Melody – fitted the bill. However, as Mel was already a single parent, I knew it would be difficult for me to cope with that, let alone sell the idea to my family. And secondly, I knew for a fact that Beauty's haemoglobin genotype was AA. With me being an AS, I feared marrying an AS because of the risk of having an SS child. Having a child with a sickle cell disorder was a risk that I was determined to avoid at all costs. I'd seen too much heartache as a result of this disorder. It's at least one of the reasons I'm an only child today.

So I'd done my homework, and saw that Beauty met my requirements on many counts. It was only after that that I allowed my love for her to flourish. I'd considered the fact that her father's ethnic group is traditionally one of the rivals to mine, but I thought that my parents were liberal enough to overlook that.

However, I hadn't counted on the fact that her mother's death soon after her birth could potentially be a problem. I wasn't willing to go back to the drawing board if I could help it.

"What is this I hear?" My father was back from his political meetings in Lagos, and had summoned me for a family one.

"About what, sir?"

"About you wanting to marry half *urhobo* half *oyibo*."

"You yourself have always said that the world is a small place."

"Yes, but it's not that small… we are not out of options."

"With all due respect, sir, it's my choice… what happened to the right to choose?"

"That's different. We each should have a right to choose our national leaders, and not have dictators imposed on us."

"But we don't have the right to choose our own wife? The person who will share the most intimate details of our lives forever?"

"You dare speak to your father in that way?" my mother sprang to his defence.

That didn't really surprise me. Being an only son, you'd be forgiven if you thought that I'd be spoilt and that I'd have at least one of my parents fighting my corner. But not so. They almost always ganged up against me. Which come to think of it, isn't a bad thing really; I turned out to be a model son. While I was growing up though, it felt really cruel.

I spent the next few days out with friends, only coming home in the small hours when everyone had gone to bed, counting the days before I returned to London, wondering what to do about my future with Beauty, whether indeed I had a future with her. And the allegations about her having killed her mother, though nonsensical, preyed heavily on my mind.

I was really unhappy that my parents would want to sabotage my choice like this, and I also knew that Beauty was estranged from her father. Although I knew I could pretty much do what I wanted, especially as I wasn't interested in the local leadership, with the hope that my parents would come round eventually, I wasn't keen on marrying without my parents' blessing. (I think I'm a bit superstitious sometimes. With the difficulties Beauty has had keeping pregnancies to full term, I've wondered whether my parents' earlier reluctance meant they still withheld some of their blessings from us. I would never admit this to anyone though, certainly not to Beauty.)

Before I left London for the Christmas break, I'd asked Beauty to marry me. I'd told her I'd ask my family to visit hers as tradition demands, and ask her father's permission on my behalf. I was hoping I'd be here when it was done, but with the hold-up from my parents, it was looking highly unlikely. In addition, I kept having these niggling doubts about Beauty's supernatural powers that may have caused her mother's death soon after her own birth, and the implications that might have for us as a family.

Through the drinking and partying, one friend asked me my plans for the future. It didn't come across as though Gbemi was being nosy. He really wanted to know because he cared about me, he said, when he noticed my hesitation. I sometimes found it unnerving, him asking such deep personal questions. This time though, I found it refreshing, as behind all the carefree jollity, my heart was heavy. So I told him about Beauty. My love for her, how I saw her to be my ideal wife, indeed a gift from God to me, and how I couldn't live my life to its fullest without her by my side. And told him about my parents' reservations about her and the conflicting emotions I've been experiencing since I discussed this with them.

And for the first time I admitted that I was angry with my father for his hypocrisy.

I also opened up to him about what I now considered the most difficult hurdle of all, and that was the fact that even if I could get my parents to come round to my way of thinking regarding cross-cultural marriages, I was unsettled about the manner of Beauty's mother's death.

Gbemi was quiet for a while. I suspect he was praying, for he was a deeply religious one.

When he spoke, it was to ask me, "You are an educated man. Is it scientifically possible for a baby to kill its mother?"

My response was a resounding "No."

"Do you remember that in our history, twins were once regarded as messengers of evil?"

"Yes?" I was tentative, not catching the connection.

"Do you realise that if twin babies were still being killed at the time of your mother's birth, you'd not be standing here today?"

"Good point, Gbemi, tell me more." I was smiling now. Of course, my mother is a twin.

"Superstitions have been around for ages. As we receive wisdom, we have a duty to future generations to expose errors by acting in truth. If you love Beauty as you say you do, and you want to marry her, I will stand by you. By all means find a way to get your parents on your side too. But certainly don't let any silly superstitions stand in the way."

As my shoulders and chest began to thaw, I made a decision right then: I'd ask Gbemi to be my best man if ever I did get married to Beauty.

It wasn't until the eve of my departure that my mother came round to my side. She said she'd been thinking about our discussion, and she could see that I really loved this girl and that I'd been unhappy since she and my father had expressed their reservations. She was going to speak to him and get him to see things from my perspective. She said she didn't want a situation where she never saw me again or her grandchildren because she and my father had been awkward when I needed their cooperation.

It was so good to hear her say that. Then I asked if she would help us bring a reconciliation between Beauty (and therefore Melody) and her father, Benjamin Iroro. I told her all about their running away to escape circumcision, and being estranged from him ever since.

"Those *urhobo-wayo* people still pursue that bush practice?" she asked with a teasing tut-tut. "Leave it to me. I know Mr Iroro, he is a reasonable man. He just doesn't like to rock the boat."

"Unlike Papa?"

"Unlike your papa before he became a chief. Now he sometimes acts like an uneducated village man. His politics and his practices often don't seem to add up these days."

I was taken aback hearing her speak like this about my father for she was usually his strongest advocate, whether he was physically present or not.

"But you seem to always be on his side," I ventured.

"For the sake of peace, my son, for the sake of peace.

But this is important to you. I will find a way to get his agreement. Remember, he is the head, but I am the neck that turns that head," she said with a smile and a demonstration of her neck turning her head this way and that.

I left home that day knowing that all would be well. And true to her promise, Mama got Papa's agreement. She liaised with Aunty Mary to work on Beauty's dad. We returned a few months later for the marriage ceremonies.

This visit, however, was different. Beauty and Mel were in mourning. I had to be strong for them. And I had to show Beauty how much I cared about her and her family. Which was why after the ceremonies I took them round various places of interest in the Warri/Effurun area during the few days we had left before returning home to London. Because even though they'd grown up in Warri, they were sheltered for the most part of it. And it was also an opportunity for Josh and Ash to learn something about their Nigerian heritage.

I simply took the greatest pleasure in being their tour guide.

September 2001
Melody

I didn't think I'd enjoy the visit as much as I did. Of course it was sad, I really was miserable, wishing Dad were alive to see my children. But I'm glad we all went along to wish him farewell. And they seemed to have enjoyed themselves. They soon learnt to yell "*NEPA*" like everyone else whenever there was a power cut – which happened quite frequently. Josh even wanted to learn to operate the generator plant which was used to supply electricity whenever there was a NEPA strike. I was relieved though that Danny wouldn't let him – he only allowed him to watch. Ash seemed fascinated by Aunty Mary's stories and Beauty's paintings from when she was at school. And they both practised speaking pidgin English to each other. It was hilarious.

Beauty seemed content to be fussed over, and Theo, well, he positively glowed when he took us on the grand tour of Warri and its environs just before we left.

I didn't take in much of Warri on the day we arrived as I was obviously blinded by grief. And for the most part, I remained at home at the old GRA (Government Reservation Area) quarters which boasted very many nice buildings that belied the awful roads that led to them. So it was quite a shock to get out into other parts of the town and see how slummy they'd become. It was heart-breaking to see houses that had been burnt down during the last ethnic conflicts. Many of them hadn't been rebuilt. A lot of the survivors moved away from mainland Warri, dispersing to the Ogborikoko, Effurun and Aladja areas.

There was still a whiff of uncertainty in the air, and even though the official 6am to 6pm curfew had been lifted, most people continued to observe it anyway. Many shops closed by 5pm and by 7pm only the very brave or the really reckless could be found on most streets. This was different from how it was when I was growing up. Warri was alive till at least midnight – not that we were allowed out that late. But we could hear and feel the buzz all the same. We could go to the night markets to get snacks like dried pork and *kpokpogari* (a type of tapioca) or edible worms, roasted corn on the cob, peanuts and *bole* (roasted ripe plantains), *kuli kuli* (a kind of crushed and balled peanuts snack) and of course *suya* (a special kind of barbecued/grilled spicy beef or goatmeat kebab), as well as local brews including palm wine and *ogogoro*.

Now, the town at night was ghost-like, reeling from the fear of 'area boys' and, unfortunately, unscrupulous police officers who could arrest you for 'loitering'. You usually had to pay your way out of it with lots of cash.

Theo still had a lot of contacts in town, and it was soon known that he was a police officer in England. So he was very comfortable keeping us out past the unofficial curfew, but not too late so Aunty Mary didn't begin to worry. Also, he encouraged Beauty to remain with us in our family compound and not go with him to his, except to visit. Although he said that it was safer for us all to remain together, I did wonder whether he needed the space to explore unsavoury haunts and former companions. I didn't breathe a word though, no point stirring up anything that would most likely end up being nothing.

The visit to the NNPC Refinery premises was rather enlightening. It was difficult to reconcile the fact that so much of Nigeria's wealth came from this area with the run-down schools and poor medical facilities that were in evidence all around us. Of course NNPC staff, especially the more senior ones, were shielded from the poverty and need that surrounded them. However, ordinary Warri residents and even NNPC junior staff could see – well, they lived – the dichotomy on a daily basis. And I could see how the seething anger could boil over into the riots that have plagued the Niger Delta area in recent years. It was good to see an angle I didn't quite notice while I was growing up here. I felt sad though that I couldn't do anything about it.

The wasteful flaring of the natural gas was another cause for complaints by the locals.

Josh seemed to be interested in the machineries and technicalities while Ash caressed the paintings, felt the fabrics used to decorate the reception area and asked such questions that many Nigerians had learnt to overlook. One was "Why is there so much fuel scarcity if fuel is produced from here?" I was happy to allow Theo to get on his socio-political soap box on that one. I must say I was surprised to notice how curious and sensitive Ash was. Why hadn't I noticed it before? She reminded me more and more of Beauty at this age, and she seemed to have a similar interest in art and textiles as Beauty did. And they both sometimes got lost in their 'tête-à-tête' as if they had forgotten there were other people with them.

It was difficult to be blind to the fuel scarcity problem that seemed to be endemic at this time. The Federal Government insisted that the scarcity was artificial. Suppliers said it was real. Caught in the middle were ordinary citizens who had to travel to their places of work and many who needed kerosene to fire their stoves to cook for their families. The queues at filling stations were long and fretful. Theo did for us what many well-off people did – sent his driver early in the morning to fill his tanks. Some even bought extra in jars as backup. Lives had been lost in accidents that happened as a result of keeping petrol in houses, as well as fake kerosene. I don't know that it necessarily stopped the practice.

Fuel scarcity though must, in part at least, explain the rise and rise of *okada* (motorcycles) as the most popular means of transportation in Warri during this period. The

interminable traffic jams and cost of other modes of transportation must also be contributing factors. Theo's sense of
adventure didn't go far enough for him to allow us a ride
on the *okada* cabbies. Josh was the only one disappointed
with that though. Personally, I was content to sit in an
air-conditioned car and watch the world through its heavily tinted windows.

Theo took us to visit a few different restaurants. The
one that captured my imagination the most was the *Point
and Kill*. This was our last outing before we left Warri for
Lagos and then on to London. Earlier in the day, Theo
had taken us to see the rebuilt Warri Central Cathedral. It
was a sight to behold – you could see it many miles away,
and thanks to the traffic jam, I had enough time to take in
its external features, from its three-domed top, its massive
and elegantly decorated windows to its heavily ornamental
doors. I hear it has a lot of fireproofed steel interiors to
protect it from arson – the fate that befell its predecessor.

This beautiful structure brought me some unpleasant
memories. My last year at school was a time when I struggled with the reality of my Christian faith. Attending a
Catholic boarding school was helpful to the extent that you
didn't ask too many questions. When I came home on holidays, I learnt that the cathedral was closed because there
had been a fight between the Urhobos and Itsekiris over
some political appointment within the church. I was still
trying to get my head around the details of how a church
that preached putting others first would fail so severely to
practise what it proclaimed, when I woke up one morning
to the news that the building had been torched. Firefight-
ers and members of the American Peace Corps spent hours
battling the blaze. Miraculously there was no loss of life –

some attributed it to the presence of Our Lady walking in the midst of the flames. But very many were injured.

Personally my injury wasn't physical. Those incidents seemed to quench whatever lingering flame of faith I had left. And I've often wondered in recent years whether my life would have turned out differently if I'd managed to hold on to my faith.

As we finished the tour of the building (the inside felt like a kingdom in its own right), I struggled with my mixed emotions. It was important to have a symbol of hope, but can the church justify spending so much money on a physical structure when so many of its parishioners lived in abject poverty? I was pleased therefore to be distracted by the drive to Big Market where we did some fabric shopping and watched Theo in his element as he haggled and bargained to get the best price possible. To finish off, Theo said some friends of his were meeting up with us at *Point and Kill*.

"What," Beauty queried on our behalf, "or where is *Point and Kill?*"

Theo, laughing, replied, "It's not a firing squad, I can assure you. Those have been done away with now that Nigeria is a democracy again." He paused for effect. "It's a restaurant."

So different was it that if I'd been blindfolded and taken there, I couldn't have told you immediately that this was in Warri. There were the welcoming smells and sight of golden palms, queen of the night and hibiscus in the well-lit premises; and the well-manicured ioxa hedges transported me back to my childhood when I used to savour sucking the nectar out of its little red flowers... I have to try it one more time...

Theo's friends were already there. As it was a cool but dry evening, we opted to take tables out on the patio, with a promise to the kids that we'd move indoors if there were too many bugs.

With the streams of jazz music in the background which later alternated with highlife and reggae, we were led to this special room where catfish and tilapia slithered and glided with just about enough water on the floor to keep them in motion. Here, we took a good look at what was available, pointed at what we wanted, it was taken expertly from the pool by hand, and killed (we didn't have to watch that step, but were welcome to if we wished). The fish were then cooked to our specifications, (hence *Point and Kill*) and served with whatever accompaniments we wanted which included snails, salad, chicken gizzards, *jollof rice, moimoi* and *peppersoup*.

I will never forget the look of fascination and awe on my children's faces as they watched the whole proceedings.

September 2001
Ashleigh (aged 12)

When Mum is happy with me, and has the time to notice me, she calls me her princess. Visiting her family in Nigeria, I got treated like one. It was just amazing. They did everything for me: served me food, cleared and washed up my dishes, ran my bath and would even have given me a wash if I'd let them. It really was cool.

I'm glad we visited. It cleared my head forever of the only images of Africa I'd had – of starving children (in north Africa) and wild animals (in the east). It was hard sometimes though, seeing hungry-looking children on the streets as we drove by in some of the fanciest cars in Warri. It was hard seeing grown-ups begging along those same streets, as if competing with the children for alms. Mum said that as there was no government welfare, anyone who didn't have somebody within their family or amongst their friends to help them was basically in real trouble.

I really enjoyed Aunty Mary's stories. She wasn't much of a one for TV. She said most of the news was bad news. Which is true over here as well. She said some of it gave her nightmares. Which is true for me also. And she said storytelling brought a family together. Well, what do I know about that? My family hardly ever sat together.

This was one of my favourites:

There was once a girl named Orinrin. She was so beautiful that when she smiled, her teeth made a ringing sound (and Aunty Mary would make this impossible-to-describe sound) *that was heard across the seven seas. Her skin was so smooth that when she rubbed on her palm kernel oil after her wash, she glowed about as bright as the full moon. She was the only child of her parents who adored her. And many men wanted to marry her. But she was very aware of her own beauty. She knew that she would never lack for suitors, and wanted to hold out for the most handsome and wealthiest man in all the known world. So she enjoyed taunting her admirers. She gave them impossible tasks and mocked them when they failed.*

One morning, she went to the village square and saw the most attractive man she'd ever set her big brown eyes upon. She knew in an instant that she wanted to marry him. So she did. And everyone agreed that she'd made the perfect choice.

At the end of the customary rites, she packed her bags,

hugged her parents goodbye and went off with her groom to his village which he said was on the other side of the sun. They had to travel through seven forests and seven seas to get there. She didn't mind, after all he was handsome and rich. And when they got to his village, she would be the envy of every girl.

After they'd travelled about a day's journey, they got to the first forest that bordered the sea. They went through the forest and on towards the sea. As they approached the sea, a voice called out, "Handsome Prince of the Seven Seas, can I have back my body part according to our deal?"

The bridegroom responded, "Certainly my friend, and thank you. Here's your leg, according to our deal." And they exchanged right legs. His straight strong leg was now replaced with a rickety one full of scabs.

This exchange repeated itself as they got to the next forest that bordered the second sea. (After the first exchange, when Aunty Mary would call out, "Handsome Prince of the Seven Seas, can I have back my body part according to our deal?" we, her listeners, would respond, "Certainly my friend…")

Eventually, the bridegroom exchanged the seven parts of his body that were borrowed – right leg, left leg, right arm, left arm, eyes, ears and nose – for his own parts, which were really ugly.

When the beautiful bride finally stopped her crying, she asked him why he had tricked her so. His response was, "I'd heard so much about you, and how you've dealt unkindly with so many. I just needed to show you that all that glistens is not gold."

She resigned herself to her fate. But he wouldn't let her stay. "Obviously you agreed to marry me because you thought I was rich and handsome. As you can see, I am neither. So I am willing to set you free from your oath, if you promise me that you will live according to what you've learnt."

"Oh I promise to live according to what I've learnt, starting with today. I can see that your soul is rich and beautiful and that is why I want to stay married to you."

And so the ugly bridegroom, who was truly a prince, reigned with his beautiful bride who remained with him. And their kingdom spanned the seven forests and the seven seas. Sometimes today, we still hear the sound that suggests that Princess Orinrin is flashing a smile...

I love the story so much that I'll look for an opportunity to use it in my creative writing class at school.

The other thing I really liked about the visit was looking through Mum's family albums. There were lots of photos of her when she was very little, and then some of her and Aunty Beauty. Mum looked so protective of her in many of those photos. That particular exercise seemed to make them both sad. In going through the pile of old photos (not every one of them made it into a proper album), I saw some of Aunty Beauty's paintings. I knew she liked to read, never knew she could paint so well.

"These are lovely, Aunty Beauty. Do you still paint?" I asked. I was surprised to see her eyes mist over.

"I haven't for a while now... hopefully I will pick it up again sometime in the future... hopefully before I'm too old to handle a brush," she smiled. And then she turned to Mum, "You remember our fantasies? I was to be a famous painter and you the greatest singer of all time?"

"Oh yes. I do. Yes."

"And we were going to be rich. We were going to have large homes in each continent. We were going to eradicate poverty. We were going to change the world,"

Aunty Beauty went on.

"Yes, I remember… we were so young… sometimes I wish I could recapture that spirit of adventure and of hope – not that I'm hopeless or anything, but sometimes I feel as though I'm stuck…"

"I know what you mean," Aunty Beauty replied. By this time I was saying in my head, "Okay…" and began to drift away…

I found some of the games fascinating, and my cousins were thrilled when I tried to learn and join in with them. 'When Will You Marry?' was an easy one. It was jumping a skipping rope to the beat of a song that goes: 'When will you marry? This year? Next year? Sometime forever… January, February, March…' and so on till you got to December. If you still hadn't stumbled, then you carried on with 'How many children will you have? One, two, three…' and so on till you eventually stumbled. And you were teased – in a good-natured way – depending on where you fell out. It made skipping really fun.

The one I found tricky to follow was called 'Ten, Ten' or 'Naught'. There was clapping, hopping and kicking the air to a count and a rhythm. The experts twirled with it as well especially when on a winning streak. You needed an opponent to play against. Or two opposing teams. Just too complicated to explain. But I learnt to play it somewhat clumsily… and enjoyed it. Apparently Mum and Aunty Beauty played it a lot as children. They said that it was like our PlayStation to them – they would rather play it than have dinner!

I didn't see much of Josh though. Apart from when we all absolutely had to be together, he was with Uncle Danny. I didn't think it possible to bond so fast with a total stranger even if they were your extended family, but Josh did, and I guess it was good for him. He got his hands dirty messing around with car engines in the name of helping Uncle Danny. He went with him to queue for fuel, to wash the car, to collect and return the marquees for the funeral, and whatever else he did while they were out. He really seemed so usefully occupied that for once in a long time, I wasn't worried about him. Mum just beamed in his direction. She never had worries about him anyway. I hoped that when we got back home, he'd continue to be that same kind and helpful Josh.

No such luck. No sooner were we back in school than he was into his usual pranks with Sam and Jerry. The latest one was them asking everyone in their class if they were ready for the maths test that day (but there wasn't meant to be one). Half the class didn't turn up as a result because they thought they might as well be absent rather than completely flunk it. And then when the teacher wouldn't postpone the lesson due to a 'lack of quorum', Josh asked him his views on the transatlantic slave trade, getting everyone into a debate about slavery still being alive and well in Britain today, and who was to blame for it. Not much maths was done in the class that period.

When he told me about it on our way home today, I couldn't help laughing. I'm so glad I am not in his class though. Call me a nerd if you like, but I really like to get on with my work.

Yes, we are back home. Josh is back to being his annoying silly self. Mum is back to being blinking blind. And me, I'm back to being the one to carry the can.

September 2001
Beauty

It was good to have gone home. It was good to have been part of the farewell ceremonies for Dad. I still can't believe that I will never see him again. It was really good to have been part of a community once more. And it was brilliant to see Theo in a more relaxed mood, possibly because he had no work issues to worry about or because he was home with his folk or just the general change of air.

Yet it is good to come back to my own home, my own bed, my own kitchen. Here, where I can get out of bed when I want, eat what I want when I want and not have anyone fuss over me (okay, a little fuss once in a while would be welcome!).

I enjoyed the visits Theo arranged for us – the cathedral, the NNPC Refinery, the restaurants (that *Point and Kill* was peculiar), the Big Market shopping and *suya* spots at night... he really seemed like he was relishing it all.

The boat ride to his homeland in the Greater Warri area though I found to be particularly hair-raising. I'd never been in a boat before, and even though I can swim, I prefer to have my feet on dry ground, thank you. However, Theo thought it was necessary for me to say thank you to his family for their support. I had seen his parents in their mainland Warri home, but to see members of his extended family, we needed to travel to his family homestead which was about 10km from the mainland. I was grateful that Mel came along to hold my hand otherwise I'm very sure I'd have chickened out at the pier.

The boats didn't instil any confidence in me. The fact

that we were renting a 12-seater motor boat for just the three of us did nothing to allay my fears. And seeing sea creatures trying to come into it just before our setting off simply terrified me. But I needn't have worried. Our captain was experienced and friendly. Once we were off, apart from the noise and the water spitting behind us, I found it relaxing. I gradually was able to let go of the railings which my pale hands had been clutching.

Although the family homestead was about a 10-minute walk from the shore, it was really easy for Theo to point it out. It wasn't a multi-storey building, but as it was surrounded by many thatched and mud huts, it appeared rather imposing in its saffron yellow, green and cream motifs.

Somehow word got out that we'd arrived because, in no time, many had come to meet us in the street, welcoming us loudly and brightly. Theo translated as much as he could and I could see from the facial expressions that they were pleased with our coming.

We were only able to spend about a couple of hours there for we needed to get back before dark. In that time though, we'd been feted with food, drinks, and high praise along with traditional music and dancing in the open courtyard.

Just before our departure, Theo's mum took me aside to one of the smaller lounge-rooms. I can see where he gets his looks – his mother's pretty face and his father's stature combined in Theo make him the specimen of a man that he is.

"You know Theo loves you, don't you?" Her kind eyes searched mine.

"Yes, Ma'am, I do. And I love him too."

"I'm glad to hear it. You know he's my only son."

"Of course I do," I replied lightly, thinking 'I have an idea where this might be going'.

"I heard about the miscarriages. I'm sorry to hear this."

"Thanks, Ma'am."

"I understand that you're tired now – you don't want to try anymore?"

"That's not exactly correct." I wished I could have been less defensive, but I'd been caught off guard.

"Are you saying that my son is lying, that you are really trying?" She spoke so softly, so sweetly. Why did that hurt me so? It was all I could do to keep the agitation from my voice.

"I haven't said that. I've said it isn't correct to suggest that I don't want to try anymore." And I hated Theo for putting me in this kind of position.

"I would want to encourage you to please keep trying. I will be praying for you."

Before I could say anything to that, Theo was at the door. "Mama, why don't you pray for us and bless us before we go?"

And so she asked God to bless us. To prosper us so that the next time we came, there would be more of us for her to entertain. She asked that the family name and title did not end with Theo. She asked God to forgive us if any of us, and she really stressed that point, if any of us had done anything wrong from when we were children that would make him withhold children from us, to forgive us, and to release his blessings in every area of our lives...

The ride back was easier. I knew what to expect this time. And my mind was working overtime following the conversation and prayer by Theo's mum. Somehow it reminded me of something Theo had said before, but I couldn't quite place my finger on it. Not wanting to spoil what had otherwise been a good holiday (apart from the fact that my dad wasn't with us anymore), I decided not to dwell on it any further. After all, I don't get to see them often, and if this was an opportunity for her to share her anxieties over wanting grandchildren, then I could afford to be gracious. And it was also possible that she'd misunderstood whatever it was Theo said to her, for surely Theo knew it wasn't for lack of trying on anyone's part.

That concern resolved on the inside, I found I was at ease enough to allow my surroundings to soak in – the sounds of the river ripples, and shoreline birds twittering; the tadpoles, sea anemones, sea turtles and other creepy crawlies edged their music into my soul. I found that I was thinking more and more of picking up my paintbrushes once again... just for the sake of it.

On the eve of our departure, Aunty Mary, in her farewell to me, said something like, "Please try oh, and don't give up, no matter what."

"Aunty Mary, what exactly are you talking about?"

"You know what I'm talking about. Children are important in every marriage. So please don't give up trying, even though it can be difficult sometimes. Theo, as you know, is an only child, and he is really worried."

"Why do you say that? He knows I'm not to blame for the fact that since the last miscarriage I haven't fallen pregnant again."

"Yes, he accepts that, but somehow thinks that if you tried harder..."

Needless to say, during the entire journey back to Lagos, and subsequently to London, I closed in on myself. I'm sure everyone had different theories as to the reasons for my withdrawal. It wasn't until we were home that Theo forced me into a conversation and it all came tumbling out.

"I've been thinking," he said, "we've had a rough year and it would be good if we had something to look forward to."

"Certainly."

"This time next year, it would be good to be holding our baby."

"You do realise that it is not down to me, Theo?"

"Yes, I do, but still, if we tried…"

"If I hear that word 'try' one more time, I won't be responsible for my reaction!"

"Come on, Beauty, calm down, control yourself. Everyone is just interested in our happiness."

"And you've been giving 'everyone' the impression that I am not trying hard enough? What do you want from me? Am I a magician? Am I God?"

"No, but if you would ask God for forgiveness, genuinely ask him, I'm sure He will act in our favour."

"Forgiveness for what exactly?"

"I don't know, but you can't have lived a perfect sinless life. When I met you, Mel was the more religious one."

"So why aren't you with Mel if that meant so much to you?"

"Because it's you I wanted. And it's you I still want. I just wish you were more accepting of your weaknesses…"

"Like?"

"Like, well, refusing to ask for forgiveness. After all, your mother did die at your birth. Could that be causing your inability to become a mum?"

Oh my God! I couldn't believe my ears. "Theophilus! Can you hear yourself at all? Is this what you really believe?"

"Not really. I just wanted us to cover all the bases, you know? I just want to prove to my parents that we've tried everything we could... I really didn't mean to upset you. I'm the one who should be asking for forgiveness. Will you please forgive me?"

What else could I do? What choices did I have? I swallowed back my bile and rolled over... looking forward to another day at work tomorrow, for my holiday was well and truly over...

CHAPTER 6

December 2001
Ashleigh (aged 12)

My hand went up in a flash. Miss didn't always choose the fastest, but today she did. I tried to hide my smile. Trace hissed "goody two shoes." Me, I squared my shoulders, threw my head back and walked to the front. It was after I got the register that I nearly ran out of the classroom. I had to make myself take slower steps as I tucked myself behind the beam thingy that blocked a part of Josh's classroom window.

Today's treat was a ball game. Josh, Sam and Jerry were sitting in three different parts of the classroom. I guess it was somebody's idea of trying to make them behave. From their seats, they were throwing the ball to one another with a dare to see who dropped it first. Mr Langley was writing on the board and moving his lips. When he turned around, everyone was still. When he turned back to write, the ball game started again. I could see some of the other children laugh. Some looked unhappy. I would have been unhappy if this happened in my class. It wasn't fun anymore. I left my hiding place and took my class register to the school office.

I'm really worried about Josh. Half the things he does, he never gets caught. Like when he put sharpener shavings into Miss Jury's coffee. Or when he put bubblegum on the teacher's seat just before Miss Begum sat on it. The whole class got punished for that one though. He told me later that he was sorry it was Miss Begum, the lovely supply who sat on it. They were expecting Miss Jury as usual that morning but she'd phoned in sick.

Then there was the day Josh, Sam and Jerry were in detention after school. Before Mr Baker got there, they had taken the hinges off the teacher's chair. Josh was suspended for two weeks. And Mum never knew.

She is so annoying, Mum is. She's like, "Oh isn't Josh such a darling? What would I do without him?"

This morning, as I rushed about to make sure I didn't forget any equipment, Josh was already waiting for me on the balcony. Mum was like, "Ash dear, please tidy up your bedroom – borrow a leaf from your big brother."

I'm like, "Yeah, right."

And she goes bright red in the face. "Hoy! Don't mutter under your breath at me, young lady!"

"Okay, Mum." I raise my hands up in the air above my head. "All I said was 'yeah, right,' and I'm running late and I don't want a fight this morning."

"Neither do I, sweetie, I was simply saying to follow Josh's example."

"Will you stop telling me that?!"

I flew out of the flat with the sound of the slammed door stinging my ears.

After Josh, as usual, went off to join his friends, my steps got slower and heavier as I neared school. I began to seriously think that maybe, just maybe, there might be something in it for me if I acted just like Josh. After all, isn't that what Mum wants?

December 2001
Melody

I don't know what's got into Ashleigh lately. Perhaps some wicked witch put a spell on her the moment she clocked 12 just over three months ago. How else can I explain the swift transformation from sweet to sour? And to think she's not even a teenager yet.

This morning, she banged the door to the bathroom so hard while I was in the shower that I thought there was an emergency and ran out to quench the fire. Only, it was Ash in a hurry to get in and just couldn't wait. When I suggested that she woke up earlier next time, she exploded, "But I can't do that – I'm waking up too early already." At 7am? I decided to drop it.

The other night I got in at about 11pm. They were both still in the living room, with the TV on and music blaring from the hi-fi. I turned them off before my kids acknowledged my presence in the room. Josh gave me his cheeky grin and a "Hi Mum, good night Mum." Ashleigh? She rolled her eyes, drew a sigh, pulled herself up to me and said, "Next time, could you at least say 'excuse me'?"

"Excuse me?"

"Yes. You don't just go around turning off something others are either watching or listening to. It's just plain rude."

"Ashleigh! Do you dare speak to your mother in that manner?"

"You could say I learnt it off you!" My hand flew to my mouth as she trotted off to her bedroom, muttering, "I have a good mind to run away from home."

Needless to say, sleep eluded me that night. Is it the absence of a father figure in her life that's the problem? Or is it the post-natal depression I suffered after her birth – is she rejecting me now for having rejected her then?

Beauty doesn't think so. She says it's only a phase which will soon pass. She says I worry too much and that if she really wanted to run away from home, Ash would not have kept threatening it... after all, we should know... no one had a clue we were planning to do a runner.

Daisy, however, says I should take the threats seriously, and to have a chat with her about the implications of running away from home. The opportunity came one evening when Josh had gone out with his friends. At the end of the six o'clock news bulletin was a missing person's appeal. I asked Ash what she thought happened to young people when they ran away from home.

"I'm not in the mood for a lecture!"

"It's just a question, Ash, you're the one giving the answers."

"Well, I'm not!"

"Ashleigh!!!!"

As she slammed shut the door to her bedroom, I could almost physically taste the bleeding in my heart...

I didn't realise I'd cried myself to sleep till I woke with a start at the sound of the telephone...

"You can't be asleep already?" the light voice at the other end teased.

"No, I didn't realise I'd dozed off."

"Everything okay?" Oh, it's Daisy. Good.

"Actually, no, things are awful with Ash and me, and... and I really don't know what to do."

"I'm so sorry to hear that. It will pass though, you

know that, don't you? She's a good kid at heart…"

"Yes, I know, but in the meantime, mine is breaking."

"Awwh! I'm so sorry!"

"No worries, I'm sure we'll be fine in the end." I don't know why I felt the need to reassure Daisy. I was the one desperate for an assurance. Still…

"Anyways, how are you? What's up?"

"I have some good news, but I don't know if this is a good time."

"It's always a good time for good news, so please, out with it, cheer me up…"

"Okay, here goes – (pause) – it's official, I'm pregnant!"

December 2001
Beauty

I know the very imperfection of my shape. Breasts that haven't yet suckled but seem to be filling up yearly – now I have to wear double D cup sizes that five years ago I didn't know existed. Love handles that I once thought were the prerogative of over-breeding simple women were now proving impervious to being hidden under my clothes, and yet, I have nothing – no one – to show for it.

Just distant memories of butterfly flutterings which I dare not savour… stronger memories of blood clots dripping down my over-embellished thighs as my body once again ejects my heart's greatest desire.

Memories of Charlie, Alex and Frankie.

Probably I'm not meant to be a mum. Doctors can't seem to find any medical reasons for the miscarriages –

or my inability to get pregnant again since I lost Frankie. 'Give it time' and 'Relax' is what they've prescribed. If only these were pills…

Anyway, I'm happy for Daisy. When she walked into *Renee's* yesterday, I kind of knew. There was a lightness in her steps, a light in her eyes and a colour to her skin that had gradually receded these past couple of years as she longed to carry her baby. And when she decided on an orange juice instead of the regular latte, my suspicions were confirmed before she'd said another word.

It was a good day at the library. The pace was slow enough for me to do some more research into the childcare course I've been thinking about for so long. If I can't have biological children of my own, it doesn't mean I can't pour my love into others', does it?

Many local colleges now do a February as well as a September enrolment for adult students. As I've missed the September window, I printed off a copy of the application form for a February entry. I've already discussed this with my line manager and they'd be willing to flex my work round my timetable.

By the end of the day, I was so excited that I couldn't wait to tell Theo Daisy's news – and mine.

His response? "There you go. Daisy's done it, not rocket science, see?"

"Erm, Theo, can we just be happy for Daisy?"

"Yes, we are. But when are we going to be happy for ourselves? There's no earthly reason why you shouldn't be able to conceive or carry to full term, is there?"

"No."

"So get on with it then."

"Why are you being so insensitive?"

"Am I? I'd think you're being oversensitive. After all, birds do it. Bees do it, even ignorant teenage girls do it. Big deal, Beauty, let's just get on with it."

And with that he grabbed my bum! What a crass brash ignoramus moron! Yet, I didn't dare say that to his face. I'm glad my thoughts are private…

So I retreated to the study. Spending the night in the same bed as him was out of the question right now. Better use the time to work on my application form.

Within an hour or so, he was at the door with a mug of hot chocolate. "Do you fancy a drink?"

"No, thanks."

"Just a little nightcap?"

"I'm fine, thanks."

By this time he'd plonked himself on a chair beside me. "Come on, Beauty…"

"Come on, what?"

"Please, let's let bygones be bygones. Let's relax with each other so we can successfully make and raise many babies."

"Theophilus, I don't have to make babies to raise them."

"I don't understand – how do you mean?"

"I'm applying for a childcare course – I'll become a childminder. That way, I can raise babies without having to make them, and at some point we can always adopt." I was so enthralled by the future that I'd momentarily forgotten his recent infraction.

"You crazy woman," he snarled, scraping back the chair, swinging out his arms which sent the mug flying. It landed against the bookshelf, baptising many of my precious books before smashing to smithereens on the solid wood floor.

"You crazy woman," he was louder this time, arms akimbo.

I opened and shut my mouth, fishlike. I could feel my eyes freeze into two big 'Os'.

"You want to give up a lucrative career to become a childminder? You would rather adopt a child than have one of your own? What's got into you? What are you thinking?"

"Hey! You are blowing the whole thing out of proportion."

"Am I? I'm the only one around here who's being logical. I'm the only one who's using their brains to the fullest capacity! You? You let your emotions run away with you… I've had enough of this. I'd rather kill myself than raise another man's child. You are such a useless woman. I would rather die first, do you hear me? Do you hear me?"

I nodded. Frantically. Of course I could hear him. Loud and clear. He was in my face, all six foot four inches of him. How could I not hear him? I shivered so much I thought I was going to go into a convulsion. I wished I would, for then I might die.

CHAPTER 7

Spring 2002
Beauty

Christmas came and went in a blur.

I don't recall much of what happened between the night that Theo threatened me with his suicide and this good April morning.

I remember feeling cold. All the time. No matter how high the thermostat was, my hands and feet were like a dog's nose.

I seem to have lived through work, through Daisy, through Mel and her difficulties.

Needless to say, I didn't complete the application for college.

I don't recall much of what else went on. But I recall Theo calling me 'useless' over and over again. I recall wanting to leave him and wanting to be with him. I recall thinking that maybe I am indeed useless if I couldn't make up my mind what it was I wanted with my life.

I recall him saying "Intelligence is not common sense – you have a lot of one but are severely deficient in the other." I recall thinking that maybe, just maybe, he was right.

I recall him saying I was selfish. That one really confused me. How could I be selfish if I wanted to give of my life to be of assistance to other mothers even if I couldn't be one? How could I be selfish if I wanted to take up a child who was given up for adoption, for whatever reasons? But then, he is an intelligent man with lots of street sense. And he loves me, doesn't he? Does he? Is there something he is seeing that I am blind to? Am I really too emotional to be logical?

I remember his explanation for why we were having more and more rows. He said his love for me had died somewhere along the line. That maybe he was spending too much time at work away from me, and so we had grown apart. But that he is working hard to revive it, and he is pretty sure that we will settle again into the love-struck couple we were when we first started dating.

I recall thinking that if I don't know what caused his love for me to die in the first place, how can I be sure it will ever be revived, and if it were revived, what would stop it from dying again? I recall wondering if he ever really loved me at all. And then deciding he must have loved me at some point – if not why would he marry me? Why would he bother whether I was reconciled with my dad or not? And why would he go out of his way to give him an outstanding in-laws' homage which is still the talk of the town in Warri? Maybe he loves me and doesn't know how to show it? Or maybe I'm too needy? Too highly strung? Too sensitive?

I remember him saying that once he puts his mind to something, he will ensure that it works. And that he has put his mind to our marriage, and therefore it will work. And that he loves me and would never again hurt me.

I recall thinking that I've been down this alleyway so many times already. Since leaving is not an option, then perhaps staying and hoping for the best is all I can do? Or maybe staying and resigning myself to the worst is more practical?

I recall thinking that I was going to go mad with too

much thinking.

And so I wanted to sleep all the time. Except when I was at work, where I wanted to cry half the time…

As the sun peeped through the cracks of my curtains this good Saturday morning, however, for the first time in a long while, I was not sad to be awake.

Spring 2002
Melody

By the end of my meeting with Josh's tutor and principal, I was once again the little girl caught with her hand in the cookie jar. Even before it started, I was already outnumbered two to one. At times like this I could kill Nick with my bare hands – he should have been here.

The office is how I remembered it to be when I did some cleaning job here many years ago. About the size of my living room and crammed with too many filing cabinets. However, it looks like someone has gone over it with a lick of paint recently, and there was no academic gown hanging from the coat hanger. That tradition seems to have gone with Mr Pullinger's retirement. Instead there was a beige fashionable mac – I would never have thought Mrs Beam would wear beige, she was more the navy/grey/black type.

"You sounded surprised, Mrs Iroro."

"Ms. You may call me Melody."

"Ms Iroro, you sounded surprised to hear that Joshua is one of our biggest bullies."

"Yes, I am, as a matter of fact. I don't see how he

could be a bully when he takes such good care of his sister."

"Ah," Mr Langley intoned, "Joshua is a good boy at home then?"

"He most certainly is." Looking from one to the other before deciding to focus on Mrs Beam, I went on, "If you'd called me in because of Ashleigh, I'd have understood that."

"Why so? She's a model pupil." It was Langley again.

"Really? She's a terror at home."

And so I spent a double period at St Katherine's High learning about my children: Ash, the straight As compliant student whose only slur was covering for Josh. And Josh, the school bully, truant and thief whose only good point was protecting Ash.

By the time I'd stalked into the flat, I'd stopped trying to wipe away the tears that streaked ceaselessly down my face.

Later that evening, I called a meeting with my offspring.

"Which of you is going to tell me what is going on at school?"

Josh stroked his invisible beard. Ash simply stared at her nails.

When she spoke, it was to say, "I've got homework due in tomorrow. That's what's going on for me. And if you don't mind, I need to go get it done." And before I could respond, she'd upped and left.

I let her go, making a mental note to pull her up on the attitude later. For now, Josh was the bigger issue.

"So, Josh, what about you?"

"What about me what?"

"Have you any homework?"

"All done."

"Can I see?"

"Hunh?

"Don't you dare 'hunh' me, young man. I want to see your homework." I was trying unsuccessfully to keep my voice firm and authoritative.

"Since when, Mum?"

Ouch! "Well, since right now."

"You've got to be kidding me, mate."

And with that, he was gone – not to his bedroom, but out of the flat.

By the time he returned at about midnight, I was in no mood to pick up the conversation, just so relieved that he'd returned all right.

Daisy's growing bun was the main light in my sky during this period. Beauty was more withdrawn than usual. I figure Daisy's pregnancy must be hard for her. But Daisy herself was glowing. The few times so far that Rob hadn't been able to attend an appointment with her, she'd asked if I'd come along, as her second birth partner. I'm so chuffed. She's confided in me that they will ask Beauty and Theo to be the baby's godparents. And that they are thinking of naming her Sunita after Daisy's ante-natal class instructor. I smiled, sure they'd have had so many other name options by the time the baby came along.

Daisy was also a good reservoir for my moans, groans and rants about my run-ins with Josh and Ash. And of course my renewed rilings about being left to raise them on my own.

Spring 2002
Theo

It is a good thing Beauty is becoming herself again. I know she's always been a moody one, but the moods seem to be coming more frequently and lasting much longer. This has been the longest yet. The baby issues may have something to do with it, but like I've said over and over again, it's just a matter of the mind. She is born to be a mother – if she puts her mind to it, it will happen.

Melody, however, is a different story entirely. I shouldn't have been surprised to hear all that's gone on with Josh and Ash. She was always so full of herself – if she'd given Nick some slack, I'm sure he'd have stuck around and that would have made a difference to the situation. Every man likes to feel that he's the best thing that happened to his woman, no matter what. Although I admire Mel's fierceness and sometimes wished Beauty would borrow some of it, I think Mel should mellow it a bit and accept the disciplinary presence of a man in her life. It would do her and her children some good.

I hate to think that Ash – intelligent, pretty and kind Ash – could go off the rails because of uncurbed rebellion. As for Josh, I meet so many of his type now that I've been moved to Neighbourhood Policing. Vital statistics as follows:

Gender – male.

Age – 14-19.

Ethnicity – black or mixed race.

Family background – single parent mum.

Status – NEET (Not in Education, Employment or Training).

Achievements – petty thievery; drug user/dealing; street terrorism; gang leadership/membership; unmarried fatherhood.

Results – drug addiction; alcoholism; imprisonment; premature death due to drug accident or overdose, drink-driving accident, gang rivalry or simply being in the wrong place at the wrong time.

The more I think about it, the more I think I should have been more involved in the lives of these children. If only for Beauty's sake.

She surprises me, Beauty, and sometimes I react in a way I am not proud of. Like the other evening. I'd had a very stressful day – not that there is ever a day that isn't stressful. One of the many incidents we'd had to deal with had to do with this delinquent who should have been in school but instead was terrorising elderly people in the town centre. And considering he wasn't yet 10 it was a bit difficult deciding what to do with him. Finally we took him home to his obviously tired mother who said she was hoping we'd arrest and detain him. I'm sure a clip round the ear would have worked, but we can't do that now; she won't do it and it doesn't look like his dad is around to do it either. So we gave him a good talking to and let him off. He promised to be of good behaviour. I'm not holding my breath…

I must still have had my head at work although my body was at home and my eyes were looking at the TV screen. I don't think I heard the beginning of her sentence, but the end bit was "… do you think Joshua will end up in prison?"

"Why?"

"Well, you would have a clue wouldn't you?"

"And what makes you think I'm Mystic Meg?"

"Why do you turn everything into a battle?"

"Why can't a man come in from work and have a rest without being quizzed?"

By now her eyes were glistening. That just gets my goat. She says, "We are a family, Theo, and families talk and listen to each other."

"And if you were listening, you would have heard that I need a break."

"Okay," she sighed. "Enjoy your break."

The rest of the evening was so quiet I wished I were at work.

I really wish she would understand the stresses of my work. Perhaps if she were fulfilled in herself, she wouldn't be so clingy. I wonder whether I should've encouraged her to go on the childcare course – that could loosen her up and help with her getting pregnant again. And when that happens, she'll go on bed rest from Day One. I'll take on any overtime going to ensure that I am able to pay for her care and the baby's. She need not worry about money. In fact, I should start doing more overtime even right now.

That's settled.

The first thing I'll do on Monday will be to pick up the application pack myself. She missed the February start but she can still get in for September. I will help her dreams come true. I can't wait for her to look on me with pleasure once again…

Spring 2002
Ashleigh (aged 12)

I don't want to be Josh's look-out anymore. After school today when he, Sam and Jerry started going to the old Indian's shop, I told him I quit. The man had just recently died. His widow looked so lost. She could have been Mum. I said how would he feel if it was Mum, and some people did this to her?

"Did what?"

"Stole from her when she was still grieving?"

"They've done so already," he replied

"Done what?"

"Stolen from her."

"Who did?"

And then he smiled that annoying 'I know something I can't tell you' smile. I stamped my foot. "Who stole from her when she was grieving? If you don't tell me then forget it! I will not look out for you! Really, I'll shop you in myself!"

"You wouldn't do that." He was still smiling.

"Why not?"

"Because you love me too much to let me rot in jail."

I hate to confess that he was right.

In under three minutes they were out, pockets bulging. I hope their teeth rot and fall out in the prime of their lives. I remained rooted to my post as they filed past. When Josh saw I wasn't following, he came back and said, "Come on then."

"You guys go ahead. I think I'll go hang out in the park for a bit before coming home – and don't save me any sweets, I'm sick to the stomach of this."

For a brief moment he kinda looked sad. Then he was back to his annoying self, grinning, "Well, have it your way. And thanks, bruv."

It's so unfair – I am not his mother.

His mother, who happens to also be my mother, she said I should have told her. That Josh was bunking off school. And mucking about when he bothered to stay. And about the letters that he never gave her. And about the nicking. About taking other kids' lunch money. About saying he would slay Sophia's dog if she didn't go out with him.

So she went mental on me. Why did that surprise me? She's always mad at me, forever complaining about this, that or the other. Even stuff that Josh does somehow manages to be my fault. So unfair.

Now she's saying that one day she'll run away from home. She can do what she wants, I can't be bovvered. I'll probably run away before her – she won't be able to leave Josh behind.

Sometimes I wished she'd just given me up at birth. Or that my dad had taken me when he left. But I'm sure he couldn't be bovvered either, else he'd have stayed.

Oh, well. Whatever…

CHAPTER 8

Summer 2002
Melody

When Esther at work first told me about the *Arise and Shine* conference, I listened out of sheer courtesy. It was one of those times when our shift ended at the same time and we walked to the bus stop together. She'd taken an interest in me when I first joined the shop team and has since kept up with the ups and downs of my life. I felt comfortable confiding in her, often feeling better just for the talking. She radiated a warmth that I found quite soothing. And she allowed me to just carry on and on and on…

This day, however, she asked me if I had anything lined up for the summer. "Apart from being available for Daisy's delivery, I'm pretty much a free woman," I replied.

"When is her expected date of delivery?"

"27th July. Why? Are you also a midwife?" I couldn't resist another opportunity to tease Esther.

"You never know," she smiled. "I'd like you to think about coming to a Salvation Army conference."

I knew she sang with the Salvation Army at Christmas and I'd attended some of their carol services, but attend a conference? No thanks.

"Think about it. You have nothing to lose. And if you gain nothing, you will at least have had a well-deserved break. Much better than running away from home." She winked with the last remark. I took the literature she handed me and promised to read it on one of those nights when sleep played 'hide and seek' with me.

And that's what I did. I merely scanned the information regarding speakers, worship leaders and workshop facilitators as none of them made any difference to me. I only knew a number of local vicars and curates, none of whom were present in this jazzy six-page A4 booklet. The trees did capture my attention though, as well as the blurb on Ashburnham Place, its history and facilities. However, what took most of my time and attention were the reviews from others who had attended in previous years.

One of the shortest testimonials read in part, 'Although many people had significant spiritual experiences, I just had simple rest for my body and soul'.

Simple rest for my body and soul. Away by myself, no children, no sister, no friends (well, apart from Esther, but she'll be busy anyway), no guys, no thinking about guys – hopefully. Just myself. The longer I stayed awake that night, the more the idea grew on me. I don't know exactly when I dropped off but I awoke with the fluorescent flyer nestled close to my chest.

Then it hit me. What about the children? I know they'd love to be home alone, and to be honest, a few months ago I'd have had no qualms in letting them look after themselves for the whole weekend. They wouldn't want to come with me, and if they did, it would spoil it for me. I went around the rest of the day like a wrung-out tea towel until Daisy came up with an idea.

"Why not send them away somewhere?"

"What, like a weekend away for each of them? That has financial implications and I hadn't quite planned for this."

"How about to friends and/or relatives?"

"Of course! But I wouldn't want to be a bother… in your condition, you don't need rebellious teenagers to give you high blood pressure."

Daisy wouldn't let me back out of it. She offered to chat with Beauty and Theo about them having Josh while she and Rob had Ash for the weekend. That way, they also would have a break from each other as together they seemed to be as thick as thieves.

"I think Beauty wouldn't mind," I mused. "But what about Theo? He can be quite unpredictable sometimes."

"I don't think he'd mind either. If it's a problem, we can find a plan B," Daisy insisted.

That was four weeks ago.

By 6pm on Thursday both couples had come to pick up their ward for the weekend.

I had never woken up to a quiet house before – apart from when they've both been still asleep. This was the first time I could remember waking up without either of the children being at home. Suddenly having the bathroom to myself for as long as I wanted lost all the pleasure I had packed into it. Is this what an empty nest feels like? As my headache intensified, I began to seriously consider cancelling the whole thing and calling for my kids to be returned home to me.

Spending some time in each of their bedrooms was meant to be an antidote. And it worked – in a different way than I intended. Josh's bedroom was a carpet of jeans and t-shirts sprawled over trainers and socks. Hardly any uncovered space on the floor, or the bed or the desk. How he manages to find his stuff, I don't know. I must pull him up on this when I get back.

I found Ash's bedroom, however, to be relaxing in her pastels and cushions and stripy bits. She still loves her Cinderellas and her delicate perfume lingered in such a soothing way – just what the doctor ordered. Sitting on her bed to extend the experience, I pick up and cuddle her pillows. Purposely inhaling her, my eyes are drawn to some scribbling on her otherwise immaculate wooden bed frame. I lean in to see better.

Line 1 said: 'Q: who do I hate more than my mother?'
Line 2: 'A: My stupid self that's who'.

I don't know how I made it from the flat to Stratford station thereafter. My fear of travelling on the tube on my own took a back seat. To Ash. My Ashleigh. She hates me. And she hates herself. Why does that surprise me? I know we've had our issues, but surely that will pass and our relationship will be good again. Is this part of the transition? Is this a rite of passage? Or is it deep-rooted? And to hate herself, poor child, she is so accomplished, so loved. Why would she hate herself?

Perhaps it's to do with her dad. I should have told her. I should have told them. I should have ensured there was a father in their lives. So really, she should hate me, and me alone. For it's me who's failed her, and Josh. And I don't know how to put it right.

The whole journey was very nearly uneventful. My train from Victoria to Bexhill through Battle was due to leave in a few minutes when I arrived at the station. I practically flew through ticket barriers, glad for having travelled light. Missing it would have meant another hour of wandering round Victoria and probably putting more shopping on the plastic that is already buckling. No, I no longer loiter in areas of temptation.

Relieved that I made it, I plugged into my MP3 player and was surprised when I awoke with a shock to see an inspector who'd obviously been speaking to me. He looked like a tired, patient man.

"Ticket please, Ma'am."

"I certainly got a ticket." I smiled to cover up my panic when a foray into my jacket pockets delivered nothing. I hoped I hadn't dropped it in my marathon sprint, I thought, as I delved into the back pockets of my combats and found it.

Whatever relief I felt disappeared when he intoned, "You've got the wrong ticket, Ma'am."

"That's not possible." I'd made it clear to the telephone travel advisor that I needed an open return to Battle, and that's what I got – and I'd given myself a pat on the back for booking 21 days early to get a good discount. What I'd forgotten to do in my hurry today was to check that I was in the right section of the train as it splits at Tonbridge. The kindly advisor had stressed this to me when he realised it was the first time I was travelling this way.

"I got a valid return to Battle. Am I in the wrong carriage?"

"Not only are you in the wrong carriage, this will take you to Folkestone. But you are also in the first class coach while your ticket is for economy."

The prickly heat inched its way rapidly from my shoulder blades, through my neck to my face. I felt like I was reeling, even though I remained seated. "I do beg your pardon, it wasn't intentional," was all I could mutter.

"I can see that, Ma'am. Unfortunately, that doesn't really matter."

"I'm sorry?"

"You are liable for a £50 fine for being in a first class coach without a valid ticket. However, as I'm wearing a black tie today, I can waive it. If it were a green one, I'd have had no option but to book you."

I mumbled my thanks, then snaked and bumped my way through six carriages to get to the right one in the midst of the tannoy announcement '…be sure you are in the right coach for your destination…'

I spent the next 25 or so minutes staring at the countryside, totally unplugged, wondering whether I'd really been saved from a fine by the colour of a tie. That was much easier than thinking about some other aspects of my life.

As the taxi from Battle station drove me through the tree-lined Appian Way into the reception courtyard of Ashburnham Place, the daunting view into infinity was tempered by the soothing smells of freshly cut grass and welcoming woods.

Summer 2002
Ashleigh (aged 12, nearly 13)

I thought she was off her rocker. I didn't want to go spend any time with anyone else, thank you. I liked my own bed. My own room. My own stuff. And no, I didn't want to take Bertie for company. Come on, where has she been?

The other option was to go with her to her camp thingy. No way. Why couldn't she just leave us home alone? After all it's just for three days. She was like, "Not an option. I don't trust either of you."

Yeah, thanks Mum. Neither do I trust you. But I only said that in my head. I didn't want another big thing. I just wanted to stay in my bedroom. If she didn't like it, she could stay home. And I told her so. We were in the middle of it when Aunty Daisy turned up.

Seeing her tummy nearly on her thighs, my heart skipped a beat. "Are you having that baby now?" She stroked her bump tenderly. "Oh no, not for another four weeks yet. Will you please come shopping with me? There's so much I need to do, time is short, it just helps to have somebody trendy help with the tricky decisions."

"What, like right now?"

"No, I'm too tired to go shopping tonight. But if you would come with me, I can show you the nursery, what's been done, what's left to do and what bits we need to buy."

I knew what she was doing. I wasn't sure if I wanted to play along. I'm getting very stressed with all the fights with Mum. And *she* never takes me shopping with her.

Just then, Uncle Theo pulled up. In full gear. He said he'd come straight from work 'cos he didn't want to have to come out again after getting in. And that Aunty Beauty was making *jollof rice* and lamb stew with *dodo* for dinner. Me, I think they planned it, so that them adults can out-number us kids.

Well, it worked. Josh came out with his flashpack, shrugged at me and off they went.

I went to get my stuff, but it took me a bit of a while as it was harder than I thought to choose what to wear for three days and three nights. Friday was easy. Blazer, top, skirt, undies, socks, school shoes, school bag – with the right books and pencil case in it. However, I'm not going to go shopping in my uniform, so I need something for

Friday afternoon, as well as Saturday and Sunday, and a spare couple of bits so I can mix and match if necessary or I can have something to change my mind for, seeing that I don't have a credit or debit card and I have to save forever to be able to buy anything trendy. Anyway… this isn't time to moan, especially as I decided not to nick or deal, so… just get on with it.

Of course I mustn't forget my pjs, sanitary towels, flannels, face wash and creams, hair stuff… Oh my gosh. I feel like a meltdown. "Mum! Do I have to go?"

"Oh Ash." It was Aunty Daisy. She's so soft spoken.

Mum was at my door in nothing flat. "You don't have to if you really don't want to, Ash. I'll just give it a miss that's all."

"Oh never mind. I'll be fine."

To be honest, I didn't want Mum to not go and then to be home with me. I wanted to be home alone. By myself. On my own. No Mum. No Josh. Just me. Which is really how it is.

As it is, going shopping with Aunt Daisy was my next best option. "Another opportunity will come," I said to myself in my head.

So, choosing a yellow and green theme, I took my time and picked my stuff, wishing there was a way I could go away and never have to return home.

———

The smell of chicken casserole greeted us as we got into Aunty Daisy's house. You'd be forgiven if you thought Uncle Rob was a celebrity chef with his toque and green-chequered apron. As he swept me in a bear hug, I suddenly blinked back a tear.

In that one moment I was hungry and happy and had forgotten that only a little while ago I was fighting with Mum.

Friday morning, Aunty Daisy made me scrambled eggs and toast for breakfast. Uncle Rob dropped me off at school before going to work. Trace saw me.

Later, as I left my table after lunch, she and Scary Spice blocked my path. "So you now ride to school, hunh, baby girl?"

I was like, "None of your business."

Not moving an inch and rocking her head from side to side, she poked a finger at me. "Do you dare talk back to me?"

"I've had enough of this," I kiss my teeth at her, trying to continue my journey. "You're not my mother."

"You little faggot, of course I'm not," she replied, giving me one heft of a push.

I fell over the table, knocked a coke bottle off it, and then landed on the broken bottle. I bled from every single pore of my body. At least, it felt that way at the time.

Just before I blacked out, I heard Scary Spice, "Where's your bodyguard brother now? Shame ..."

When I woke up later at Newham General, Aunty Daisy was as white as my sheet. She lit up when she saw my eyes, and I could tell she'd been crying. "Hey Aunt D," I stuttered, "I'm okay, don't worry."

She took my hand in both of hers and pressed it against her cheek. "I'm terribly sorry."

"Hey! It's not your fault!"

"I'm supposed to be looking after you."

"How could you have prevented this?"

"I don't know. Perhaps advised you to be careful? Possibly homeschooled you?"

I couldn't help laughing, "For one day?"

"I don't know, Ash. If I can't keep you safe for 24 hours, what will I do about Sunita? Babies can't speak, how will I know what she needs? How can I keep her safe and secure?"

Oh! I see. "I can help, if you would let me."

"Would you, Ash? I know you are only young but you are such a capable and clever girl. Sometimes I fear I will mess things up. I don't think I can be a good mother – ouch!"

"What? Are you okay?"

She flashed the weirdest contorted smile ever. "I think Sunita is on the way."

Summer 2002
Beauty

I'd eaten too many rice cakes. And I felt like being sick.

This was new.

Normally I either lost my appetite completely and only ate for survival, or found it to be so rich that I had to bargain with myself to stop stuffing. That's why I had healthy snacks in the cupboard so when that craving seized me, I would at least be eating popcorn rather than crisps, and rice cakes rather than chocolate digestives. Not that they seem to make any difference as far as my dress size is concerned.

I'd never felt like being sick, no matter how much I'd eaten.

What kind of example would I be to Josh? I'd jumped at the chance to be there for Mel. But I didn't stop to take stock of how it would impact me, of how I would actually be responsible (okay, only in part) for a 14-year-old boy whose head teacher has promised never to give him a positive reference.

Although I'd been part of his life all along, I soon realised that the only thing I knew about him was that he loved *jollof rice* and *dodo*. Hence my choice for dinner. But I should have paid more attention. Mel was doing a good job, all by herself. We should have been actively involved with her. After all, sharing the same DNA is not what makes you a sister, neither is sharing experiences, late night chitchats or even the commonality of faith. I cannot stand apart and still be a sister to Mel.

My hand was making its way again to the pack of rice cakes when Theo and Josh walked in, obviously in the middle of a heated debate which carried on for most of the evening. If I were to give it a title, it would be 'One man's terrorist is another's freedom fighter'.

They were quite a pair to watch, Josh and Theo.

"You say it's better to be safe, Uncle Theo."

"Yes, better safe than sorry."

"Would you say anyone was safer following the unlawful police killing of Jose de Souza?"

Leaning forward intently, Theo said, "Hey, it was an accident. The intention, however, was to prevent a terrorist bomb attack on the capital. There'd been so much pressure following the 9/11 attacks in New York. In that respect, one man died for the safety of potentially thousands of others."

"Isn't that a bit rich? What if it was me?"

"It couldn't be you, come on."

"But, let's just pretend it was. Would you be satisfied that it was an accident? That your colleagues couldn't tell a potential killer from a regular bloke just because of the colour of his skin? And they couldn't tell the difference between the denim jacket de Souza wore and the bulky black one they reported that he had on to cover a device?"

"Point taken. And a good one too."

It was good to hear Theo lose an argument to a lad.

"So what are you planning to study then?" Theo queried. "Law?"

Josh shrugged and excused himself.

The next morning, I was surprised to find Theo lingering with toast and coffee at the breakfast table. He was usually in a big rush to go save the world.

I guess he was practising what he'd been saying recently about trying to save his family first.

After Josh had gone to bed, we'd lingered late into the night. We'd talked a lot, like the good old days. He'd said he'd be happy to grow old with me whether or not I gave him children. That he'd consider a career change so he could spend more time with me. That although adoption wasn't on the agenda, my childcare course was. He would be happy to open up our home to a patter of tiny feet if that would make me happy.

"Are you sure?"

"Of course I am. I couldn't be surer."

And with a flourish, he pulled out an application pack from the local college. "Go ahead and pursue your dreams. My dream is to make your dreams come true," he said, taking a mock bow before handing me the pack.

Ah, I was all buttery on the inside, long distant and

familiar feelings of love and joy welling up and overflowing… the ecstasy was real. His tenderness was touching. The man I'd married had returned.

I knew it wasn't all a dream because the application pack was by my bedside table in the morning. And Theo was at the breakfast table. There was hope yet for our relationship.

CHAPTER 9

New Year's Eve 2003 (31ˢᵗ December 2002)
Theo

The one thing I've missed since my promotion has been pounding the streets. Therefore, I welcome tonight. Simon and I stroll up and down Oxford Street, a boulevard of lights, an avenue of people. The relative calm is oftentimes overshadowed by the excitement echoed by revellers in various stages of undress and intoxication.

Simon and I seem to be joined at the hip as far as our walk in the Met is concerned. We were in the same training set in Hendon and have worked in the same division most of the time. Although he is now in charge of Policies and Procedures, he also welcomes the opportunity to walk the streets.

"It seems like a regular night for a New Year's Eve," Simon offers.

"It does, doesn't it? No excitement, no drama, no trauma. Just plain raining. Not that I'm complaining."

Actually, that is the synopsis of my life at the moment. Beauty has cheered up a great deal since she started her childcare course in September. She even made me a packed lunch/dinner as I got ready for work today, happy – at least, content – to be home alone on a New Year's Eve. She didn't want to go to Mel's who was going for a midnight service at her church.

Mel. Now she's a bit of an enigma these days. If I didn't know her better I'd be worried. Since she came back from her camp in the summer, she's been different. She's been carrying on about "Jesus' love is wonderful and unconditional." My question is, if this were so, why is she working so hard for it? When she's not at work, you can be sure she's in church for one activity or another. She's so totally consumed by him, I'm sure there won't be room for any other guy in her life – actually, maybe that's the whole point. Who knows with women?

"Shall we stop by the *Kings Arms* for a glass of lemonade?" Simon cuts into my musings.

"I don't see why not. It's still a couple of hours before midnight."

We walk the few hundred yards to the alleyway shortcut to the pub. We hear the commotion before seeing it. With a silent nod, we acknowledge the loss of our lemonade and sprint towards the crowd, Simon reporting the scene and our intentions to the station who promised standby and to send us backup if necessary.

We have to hack our way through the crowd which was intent on the free live entertainment. The two lads engaged in the brawl carry on in spite of our loud orders for them to break it up. We have to pull them apart physically to restrain them. Simon has the lanky white young man, not a day older than 15, who is bleeding from his forehead and swearing profusely while I get the mixed-race one of about the same age who is fighting a losing battle of trying to wrest himself from my grip.

After cuffing his hands behind his back, I turn him around as I read him his rights and freeze: Joshua.

January 2003
Beauty

Theo has gone too far this time. I know he thinks he is better than me – even if he is, he does not have any right to be rude to me and about my family.

I thought we'd had it cracked. I thought we'd turned the corner in our relationship and that as we were now more in harmony, the chances of my conceiving and keeping the pregnancy would be higher. After all, he changed his mind about the childcare course, and even though he's been complaining lately that I'm studying too much (hello! I have assignments to complete, and I am working full time while studying this part-time day release plus two evenings a week); I put it down to a lack of understanding on his part on what it takes to complete an *Early Years Care and Education Certificate Course* successfully. He probably expects it's child's play.

When he went off to work doing both his regular shift and overtime during the Christmas and New Year period, I willed myself to adopt a positive outlook – after all, he was working hard and not goofing off in a pub getting drunk or visiting seedy nightclubs (except in the line of duty one would hope). I wore a cheerful countenance for him, not wanting to add to his stresses.

He comes in from work on New Year's Day overcast like an impending African thunderstorm. I knew once he crossed the threshold that only a miracle would prevent a deluge. I hoped for a divine intervention, as Mel has been telling me all things are possible to him – or her – who believes.

"Happy New Year, sweetheart." I tiptoe to kiss him on the lips. The next thing I know I'm on my backside on the floor.

"What's that for?" I query from the depths of my shock.

"I'm not in the mood; I've had a rough night."

"You're not in the mood for what? You're not in the mood to be civil?" By now I'd dragged myself up to my feet, refusing to show him how sore I was.

"I say I am not in the mood – when I pound the streets of London trying to keep them safe, I do not expect to receive insults."

"But you know it comes with the territory."

"I didn't know my own nephew would be part of the insulting and assaulting brigade."

"Your nephew?"

"Actually, your nephew. No nephew of mine – if I had any – would dare behave like that."

"Theophilus, I need to hear what you're saying." I'd given up trying to hide my exasperation. "Please speak plainly."

"Speak plainly? I will speak plainly – I arrested Joshua last night, yes, Joshua, your nephew, your sister's son. He split somebody's head. He's right now in detention."

"Why didn't you just say so? Does Melody know?"

"Because, like I said, I am not in the mood to have a conversation with spoilt brats."

"What are you being so rude to me for? I am not Joshua."

"No, but you might as well be – you are spoilt, Melody is spoilt, who instead of looking after her children is spending all her time in church. If your father had been firmer…"

"Don't even go there," I sigh and slump on the sofa.

"I will go wherever I please. If he had done a good job of bringing you all up properly, Josh would have turned out differently. I tell you now, no child of mine will be molly-coddled, irrespective of the circumstances of his birth…"

He was bending over me, yelling and jabbing his forefinger… I soon ceased hearing the words having folded my head into my arms and balled into my favourite foetal position, and tucking myself into the furthermost part of the chair.

January 2003
Melody

My heart crash-landed into a million fragments. My son. My baby boy. Is in detention. He will probably be charged with – ABH? GBH? What if the person dies? Oh my God! He'd then be a murderer. And I, a mum to a murderer. How did I let this happen? Oh my God!

I'd gone to Daisy's after seeing in the New Year at the Salvation Army Church of Christ. Ash didn't want to come with me but was happy to go to Daisy's. Josh said he'd go out with his friends, promised to be sober, clean and careful – how foolish I've been. How could I have let him go off on his own? And on New Year's Eve too?

When I got in at about 1.00am, they were all still awake, with Sunita crawling everywhere, behind and in between crevices being her favourite spots at the moment. At Rob's invitation, we stayed the night. Ash was lost in her DVD marathon. The rest of us just lounged in the front room. Sunita, bottom-shuffling, got to Daisy's leg and tried to pull herself up, babbling what sounded to me like "mam ma, mam ma!"

"She's such a fast child," I said, pointing out the obvious, "attempting to stand up already."

Daisy simply stared.

"A penny for your thoughts, Lady D."

She smiled, "Simply daydreaming that's all."

"Okay then, a pound for your dreams."

"Maybe... one day... see you all later..."

And then she left us to it. Rob sighed, shrugged, picked up Sunita and began bouncing her on his knees, causing her to roll in fits of giggles.

"She'll be all right, you know that," I said, nodding in the direction of Daisy's exit.

"How can you be so sure?"

"Because I've been there." I was glad that Ash was out of earshot as I went ahead and shared with Rob the long dark shadows that had engulfed my world from the moment of her birth.

Anyway, this was why we weren't home when Beauty walked down to my flat that New Year's Day to tell me about Josh. She eventually got me on the phone – and I asked why she hadn't called in the first place. She said she needed the walk to clear her head. It was after she'd told me everything that I saw why she needed that head-clearing walk.

That was two weeks ago. I haven't yet been able to clear my own head. Or to stitch back the pieces of my splintered heart.

Joshua, my baby Joshua, is now a jailbird. Why Theo felt that was necessary, I don't know... maybe flexing his muscles made him feel good with himself. At least he looks after Beauty – that is something I can be grateful for.

And Ash? Well, she wouldn't speak to me. Not about things that matter anyway. I guess she still hates me. Can I blame her? I haven't told her certain things that matter. Only to protect her heart though. Yet, she does have a right to know. They both have a right to know. Actually, they all have a right to know. I just wanted everyone to be happy. And now I've managed to make a miserable mess of everything.

If Nick (or anyone else for that matter) wanted to leave, I wasn't going to force him to stay. Was I wrong in this? Should I have fought for my children to have had a father? Should I have tried harder to marry or to at least get into a more permanent relationship? Would that have given them the stability they needed to have a regular childhood? What will become of them? Is Josh going to keep getting into trouble with the law? Is he going to be reserved a cell in the prison? I know he promised me he'll turn his life around, but how can I be sure? And Ash, is Ash going to keep socialising only with people who are either too old or too young for her? Is she going to keep locking me out? And even if she eventually opens up to me, will I have anything worthwhile to impart to her?

Will I ever be able to mend my broken heart? Will I have another opportunity to mother these children right?

Sacred Heart of Jesus, have mercy on me.

CHAPTER 10

I can't believe that Sunita is one.

I can't believe Josh is taking out the rubbish off his own back.

And I can't believe I'm in love.

Aunty Daisy says they always come in threes – your bus, after you've been waiting for a long time, turns up three in a row; like getting caught out in the rain on the day you had your hair retouched, your clothes out on the line and a car splashes all over you even though you tried your hardest to dodge it. They come in threes: bad stuff (I've had loads and loads of those) and obviously good stuff (I'm just beginning to see some of those).

It's kind of weird that good stuff began to happen to me when things were really awful – Josh had had a taste of the inside, I was bullied and ended up in hospital, and while there, Aunty Daisy went into labour to have Sunita.

Nathan and a few other kids from school came to see me in hospital – which was a surprise as not many spoke to me or even acknowledged my existence. I did catch Nathan eyeing me from time to time, but I didn't think he would be interested in me – why would he? He was the Zack Efron of our school and all the popular girls including Trace and Scary Spice were always hanging out with him.

To be honest I thought I was dreaming. This was

day three – Sunday. Mum wasn't yet back from her camp. Aunty Daisy thought it was best to let her enjoy her first weekend away alone, ever, as any news of the drama will cause her to cut it short. I'd stopped bleeding. I wasn't feeling as sore, but the welts on my legs were still very ugly. I'd been allowed to cuddle Sunita – the first and only newborn I've ever seen close up. Aunty Beauty, Uncle Theo (who fumed so much that I felt sorry for Trace and Spice) and Josh had all been to see me. So when at about 7.30pm the nurse popped her head round my curtains to say, "Visitors," I thought it was Mum. It wasn't until Nathan and his crew that included Trace and Spice, of course, trouped in that I began to fret about how pathetic I looked in this retard floral hospital gown, hair kinked out, face unmade and oh, I wanted to be anywhere else but here.

"You alright, mate?" Tracy spoke first.

I could only nod while thinking: 'Mate?' Did she just call me 'mate'? Not 'loser', 'crack head', 'hybrid' but 'mate'?

She went on, "I'm really sorry, I didn't mean to hurt you."

"And I'm sorry too," Scary Spice joined in. "Is there anything we can do to help?"

It was all I could do to stop the tears from spilling. Then Nathan spoke up, "She looks tired, we should probably come again tomorrow after school, is that okay, Ash?"

"Thanks, guys," I nodded.

They left me with a card signed by everyone in our class. Nathan then gave me a little package and leaned so close to my ear I could have fainted from his aftershave. "Open it later, it's from my heart to yours." I was surprised at the sudden flurries that went on in the pit of my tummy.

Later that night, when I couldn't sleep for wondering

when I would see Mum again, if ever, I opened the package. I didn't understand why my hands were shaking. It was a snow globe with the background picture of a robin and a bluebird both perched on a snowladen fir tree...

Apparently Mum didn't hear about my accident or Sunita's birth until she spoke with Aunty Beauty on Monday morning. She swept into Newham General like a hurricane and it didn't matter that visiting time wasn't till 4pm. I never knew I'd be so pleased to see her.

And to think this was a year ago.

Since then, Nathan and I have become an item.

Summer 2003
Melody

Sunita is one. Wao! I'm so sorry I missed her birth. Yet, in a way, we are twins, for while she was being born at Newham General, I was being reborn at Ashburnham. And it really has been a year since that eventful weekend.

I remember the journey back. I was so full of energy (the rest had been good for me), and a vision for the future that was brighter than I could ever remember experiencing. I'd never been to a Christian conference before and I didn't quite know what to expect. It certainly was different from church. The leaders seemed like ordinary people who were struggling with normal life matters just like the rest of us.

What really began to tug at my heartstrings was when Lisa Holdden began to speak about the Father Heart of God. I had never heard a thing like that in my life. She spoke about God as Father who provides for, protects and guides his children; as one who never wants them to be orphans; as one who is pleased with them, plays with them and rejoices over them with singing.

And then she spoke about the Mother Heart of God, the God who nurtures, comforts and heals his children. He 'kisses it better', would go to the wall for them – and he did, he went to the cross to die in their place.

It completely threw me. God was personally interested in my life, wanting to be there with me, to be an active parent to me, if I would let him. After the tears subsided, I chose to invite him to do just that. One of the ministers prayed with me. I felt warm and tingly all over. And as she continued to pray for protection and safety for my children, the tears came tumbling down once again. It wasn't till I spoke with Beauty on Monday morning that I realised that at about that same time, Ash was in hospital, in a coma.

By the time Ash was discharged from hospital a week later, she was less antagonistic towards me. In the last few months, however, watching her grow in her relationship with Nathan, and separately with Sunita, I can see a new level of maturity in her, and I am hoping that our relationship will get to the point of being comfortable, at the very least.

I have failed her in so many ways. I should have been there more for her in a way that my mother wasn't for me. I think in a way she had it worse than me; at least the reason my mother wasn't there for me was that she had died. In Ash's case, I've been too busy with the demands of life that I've been content that she was okay with Josh. And my dad, at least he was physically there. Hers isn't. And I am mostly to blame for that. I pray she is able to forgive me one day... as a matter of fact, I pray that I am able to forgive myself...

I pray also that Joshua is able to forgive me. I remember going to get him after posting his bail, still angry with Theo for putting him in the holding facility when he could easily have taken custody of him personally.

After completing all the paperwork, the wait became unbearable. The place was so hot and stuffy I wondered when the windows were last opened, if ever. I was reading one of the 'Polite Notices to Visitors' for the 100th time when the sergeant called me and said, "Here for Joshua Iroro?"

"Yes please, he's my son."

"He's a good one," he said, and winking at me he went on, "we don't ever want to see him here again."

"Thanks," was all I could say, blinking back the tears.

The journey home was a silent one. I knew I couldn't trust myself to speak – either I'd cry or I'd rant, neither of which I wished to indulge in at that point. Josh only used few words with me naturally anyway. So the radio filled up the space between us.

He offered to make me a cup of coffee when we got home. I declined it without thinking. Then he asked if there was anything I needed. I said, "No thanks, Joshua, I just want to rest."

That was when he broke down and cried. Like he was once again my little three-year-old boy. I gathered him in my arms and just let my own tears roll.

When it was all done, he took both my hands and said to me, "Mum, I'll never do anything to cause you any more unrest. I promise."

I said nothing. I wanted to believe him. But I couldn't.

And I kept fretting until the day a letter came and I realised that he had applied for and got a place in a college to do an NVQ in *Mechanical Engineering Services - Plumbing (Domestic)*.

Anyway, summer's here now, Sunita's one and her beach party was perfect. For starters, it didn't rain. It was a risk Daisy was willing to take. She didn't want a house party. She didn't want a 'functions room' party. She really didn't want any party at first. The past year had been difficult for her. She didn't seem to get over the initial baby blues, and quite often when I'd spent time with her, she sort of reminded me of myself in the months following Ash's birth. Although she didn't tell me, I could tell when she'd been crying – and it seemed to be often.

She would hardly hold Sunita except to nurse her, and was eager to hand her to Rob or anybody else present or place her back in her cot. She seemed to be anxious over the most insignificant of issues but lacklustre about things that ought to matter. And she seemed to have lost all interest in her personal appearance. She'd not yet restarted her weekly lunches with Beauty and I know that Beauty missed those.

She seemed to want to sleep all the time and still said she was tired when she got out of bed. Rob was very supportive and I really wished I'd met somebody like that. Ash was eager to babysit Sunita and seemed to have been present during all the milestones, from first smile to first steps. I accompanied Daisy to health visitor/GP surgery trips whenever Rob couldn't. She couldn't bear to hold the baby for her jabs.

I don't know what I would have done if I hadn't recently discovered I could talk to God about anything. I found I talked more about things that bothered me – like wanting Daisy to be happy again; like wanting things to be right between my children and me; like wishing Beauty would get pregnant again, and this time carry to full term.

And when Daisy eventually agreed to a party for Sunita, albeit at Southend-on-Sea, I talked to God about keeping the rain at bay. And he did. Good one!

Summer 2003
Beauty

I am so tired these days. Honestly, I'm experiencing levels of exhaustion I didn't even know existed. The only new thing to my schedule is the *Early Years* course which I am enjoying apart from when Theo is off work and begins to complain that I'm spending too much time on my assignments.

Last night when he went a-moaning again, I explained to him that I needed to meet the deadlines, and that I needed to pace myself so I'm not too exhausted. He turned his back on me and muttered, "Lazy bones."

Although he said he was joking, I did wonder whether there was some truth to it. After all, I do seem to find everything that much more difficult than other people.

I remember though, the first time he called me 'lazy'. The first time, that is, when it really cut me to my marrow. I was pregnant for the first time, with Charlie. This was the one that went the longest. Only a couple of weeks more and it could have been a prem, and could probably have been saved.

I threw up from even before I knew I was pregnant. I had dizzy spells, lost my appetite and could hardly keep awake, and then later I could hardly get to sleep. Of course Theo was careful to point out to me that pregnancy was a thing of joy, and that I wasn't sick, just pregnant, and that if he could, he would have borne the pregnancy for me, but he couldn't so I just had to get on with it. And I did. Or at least so I thought.

We were still living in the flat then, on the second of six floors. I couldn't stand the smell and confinement of the lifts. As time went on, I avoided going downstairs except when I had to, and once out, I did absolutely everything I could think of that needed doing before coming back into the flat.

We didn't have a tumble dryer in those days. And Theo didn't like the idea of wet clothes on the radiator or even on the airer inside the flat. On this particular Saturday morning, I had done the washing early, hung it on the airer which I'd placed on the balcony, with the towels draped over the balcony railings. At about 10am, I began to feel sleepy again so I went in for a nap.

Only to be awakened with a gust of cold air.

"Hey! Why did you pull the duvet off me?"

"To let you know how unhappy you've made our neighbour downstairs," was his mysterious reply.

"I don't believe this," was all I could manage, for Theo was in a torrent. Apparently he'd been stopped as he came home from his shift this morning. The elderly widow in the ground floor flat right under us pulled him in to show him where drips from our balcony were decorating hers, and she wasn't too pleased.

"So, she's unhappy?"

"Yes, she is, and I don't like upsetting my neighbours."

"But you don't mind upsetting your wife? Do you know how many hours I slept last night?"

"Do you know how many I slept? Zilch! I want to come home to some peace and quiet, not to be being waylaid by Mrs Grouchy made further grumpy by my lazy no-good wife. Sometimes I wonder what I did wrong to be lumbered with you."

By this time, he was divested of his uniform, robed in his pyjamas and under the duvet.

I cannot begin to tell you how much that hurt, and all that followed. Yet, I've got to find a way to leave the past well alone. It somehow has a way of creeping up on me. I need to deal with today, the here and the now, or at least the more recent stuff, things that bring a smile to my face, and a hope to my heart. Like Daisy.

Seeing her during Sunita's first birthday party was such a joy. She seems to have turned the corner. I would never have imagined Daisy to be at risk of post-natal depression – she and Rob had both wanted a baby for a while; they are financially stable; they have a good home; her career is well established and she could pick it up whenever she wanted. She has so many options. Frankly, there were times when I felt like shaking her up to tell her to look and see how lucky she was... Aunty Mary would have done that... not that I know if it would have worked in this instance, but she is bold, Aunty Mary. I'm just a shrinking violet, a wilting willow, a wimp. For once though, I'm glad I kept my thoughts to myself.

I thought the setting was radical. There is nothing like the seaside to bring out the child in everyone, including Theo. From about 2.00pm when we met up till about

6.00pm when we had a fish and chips supper followed by the cutting of the cake at the *Hammer Head*, it was fun and laughter galore.

There was only one thing that caused me a bit of bother – the way Nathan was with Ash. He followed her everywhere and too closely for my comfort. He completed her sentences and answered questions directed to her. He referred to her as 'babe' (which irritated me – she's neither a baby nor a pig) and there was something about his sleekness that knotted my guts.

Yet, Ash seemed happy, as did Mel and everyone else. I went to bed that night uneasy, trying to grasp what caused me such great discomfort, an unease that was so familiar yet so elusive...

I woke up with a start that night, with the word 'smothered' on my lips. And a memory of me saying to Mel many years ago, "Mel, I love Theo so very much, but sometimes I feel smothered."

As the hand of fear disengaged itself slowly from my heart, I awakened with a realisation that I had to do something about it, for Ash's sake.

But what could I do? What could I say? That would make sense anyway? I gave it a go, and spoke with Ash. Of course she laughed me off as being overprotective. "He is really cool, Aunty B," she insisted. "He really looks after me. I know he loves me."

"But he doesn't let you look after yourself, does he?"

"He feels it's a man's responsibility to look after his lady, and it does kind of make me feel good."

"And he speaks for you. If that happens for long enough, you will lose your voice – and along with it your confidence, even your own identity. Ash, he's not safe."

"Being married to a copper has made you extra suspicious," she insisted. "He is very safe, but thank you for looking out for me. You are the greatest aunt in the whole wide world."

I had to let it ride. But the thoughts would not leave me alone. I decided to raise it with Mel who told me nicely to just bugger off and leave them well alone.

So I did. Knowing that if somebody had tried to warn me off Theo, I wouldn't have believed them. Knowing that if I'd had information on how to read the signs then, I'd probably have understood it better and been more cautious. Knowing that I will keep seeking opportunities to pass on relevant information to Ash in the hope that she will discover the truth for herself, and flee while she still can… But then, what if I was wrong? What if my anxieties are colouring my judgement? I decided then it was best not to meddle.

When the leaflet came through the door, with all the pizza offers and minicab numbers, I knew I had to make the phone call in the first instance. What caught my attention was the question 'Are you in an abusive relationship?' I took a closer look.

Are you in an abusive relationship?

Do you know of anyone who might be?

Discover the truth about **Domestic Violence** (which includes Physical, Verbal, Emotional, Financial and Sexual Abuse) and empower yourself to stop it in your life and/or in your community

Domestic Violence is more widespread than reported, cuts across all classes, races and creeds and its wounds cut deeper than meets the eye

Are you a victim? Do not continue to suffer in silence

Are you unsure? Why not find out?

For further information on support available in your area, call our confidential 24hour support line……………..

Be safe. Be aware. Take care

AADV+VA
(Action Against Domestic Violence and Verbal Abuse)

I couldn't tell you how long I took poring over that little leaflet, a torrent of questions which really were variations of: *I couldn't be in an abusive relationship, could I? Theo's a good man, he never hit me. Not really. But the words, surely, they are just words? And I'm a sensitive one, aren't I? Somebody strong like Mel might take it on the chin and give back as good as she gets. Surely I would know it if I were being abused?*

Yet… I had to find out… And if it turns out I'm okay, and that my problems with Theo were just relationship issues, then at least I can focus on trying again for us to attend marriage counselling. And what I learn might be useful for somebody else. After all, I am a librarian. So, a few days later, I plucked up some bottle, called the number, and booked myself on an initial consultation. The high level of confidentiality that covered the whole thing suited me just fine.

After that initial session with the women's support worker, I couldn't say for sure that I was in an abusive relationship. Do you know what alarmed me though? It was the fact that I couldn't say for sure that I wasn't. I thought to follow her counsel and get a trusted 'outsider's' opinion. I eventually broached the topic with Daisy.

"Would you know if you were in an abusive relationship, Daisy?"

"I would hope so – after all, I'd be carrying the bruises around."

"What if it wasn't physical, how could you tell?"

"That I do not know. Why do you ask? Do you think I'm being abused?"

"No, I think I am."

"Really? By who?"

"Theo."

"Are you sure, Beauty? He puts abusers away, surely he's not one of them?"

"I know," I nodded, looking intently into my cold coffee as if for some clues. "I know he's a good man, and a good police officer. My *confusionitis* must be getting clinical." I tried to shrug it off in a chuckle, which didn't quite come out right.

Daisy was listening. Really listening. I know this because of what she said next, "Why do you say that? You are one of the most lucid people I've ever known."

I opened my mouth. But shut it straight away as I could feel the response rush to my eyes. Dear Daisy. Her hug was soothing. Firm. Comforting.

As we parted company and I made my way home, the knotting on my insides started again, getting tighter the nearer home I got. I knew for sure that something wasn't quite right. What I didn't quite know was exactly what was wrong.

CHAPTER 11

Summer 2004
Beauty

She could easily have been mine. Sunita, my little princess, my goddaughter, the closest I've ever had to a child of my own. I hear the pattering of her footsteps in my dreams sometimes, the dimpled cheeks that offer me a cheeky smile after she's melted my heart once again and I've given her more treats than I'd intended; the little chubby fingers that touch my lips softly with such sincerity that I've been known on occasion to wipe back a tear… I see her and other little ones in my dreams and then I wake up… and I try to go back to sleep again to continue it… but it never quite works out that way.

I have learnt to make up for such interrupted visions of the night. On purpose I see her in my mind's eye, and summon up scenes from our times together. For instance when she plays with my fuzzy wuzzy dirty brown hair – she seems to prefer it to her teddy bear. And I hear her at the end of *The Tiger Who Came To Tea*, whining, "Again please, Aunty B, read it to me again." And I smile when I recall how she breaks into hysterics even before I get to the 'tickle you under there' part of *Round and Round the Garden*.

When Daisy announced late last year that she was going back to work in January, I knew I had to offer her my childminding services.

"Are you sure you want me to be your employer?" Daisy queried.

"Would you rather hand Sunita to a total stranger?" was my comeback.

We were having our weekly lunches again, but these days at *Kids' Domain*. At this precise moment, Sunita was romping about in the ball pit. We both turned in her direction in almost perfect unison.

"No, Beauty. It would be an honour to have you look after Sunita for us. Thank you."

"The pleasure, really, is mine. I will care for Sunita as if she were my very own – after all, I am her godmother and it's about time I took my duties a bit more seriously."

Giving up my work at the library was more difficult than I'd envisaged. As God would have it, it turned out that they needed to make some cuts and were offering a voluntary redundancy package. If they didn't have enough volunteers, they'd have to make compulsory cuts. I thought £35,000 was sweet enough to help me bite the bullet, and to keep Theo satisfied that it was a good decision. And it did.

What came as a surprise was his reaction to my taking on Sunita.

"And the reason you want to babysit Sunita is…?"

"To begin my childminding business once I finish with the library job."

"And you want to do this because…?"

"Because having completed the *Early Years* course, I have several options, childminding being the most suitable for me right now."

"I'd have thought an intelligent woman like you would have wanted to do something more mentally stimulating than childminding." How can I describe to you the sneer in his voice? Or the utter contempt that oozed from his face?

"Theo," I pulled myself up to face him as far as I could, on tiptoes and all, "you are insulting my intelligence. I demand an apology."

"Woman! Are you drunk or something?"

I decided to take my time to respond. It was almost as though I were seeing him for the first time. Is this really Theo, my Theo, or is somebody else impersonating him?

My silent stare must have made him uncomfortable. As he began to retreat into his easy chair, I surprised myself when I called out, "I'll take the 'or something'. And I will let you know now that I will no longer accept your rudeness to me. I am a grown woman, I can make decisions. You don't have to agree with me, but you surely have no right to insult me."

I didn't hang around to hear his response. He spent the rest of the evening like a bear with a sore head.

It's been six months now. I haven't taken on another child – I haven't even advertised my services. I'm happy to stick with Sunita for now – the only one who knows that I've been attending the Action Against Domestic Violence and Verbal Abuse (AADV+VA) Support Centre every Wednesday afternoon.

After the initial consultation where I'd left feeling even more confused than before; after I'd broken down trying to discuss it with Daisy, my trusted objective 'outsider'; after I couldn't decide whether I was being abused or I was just plain clinically confused, I decided to attend the small group support sessions. I thought that being in that setting would bring me some clarity one way or another. And I was convinced that even if the discovery was not useful to me personally, I could use it to help somebody else.

There were typically a maximum of eight ladies in a group with a support worker and her assistant. The meeting venues were in two or three different places which were kept highly confidential. I found it suited me fine and it was extremely convenient that we could attend with our own preschoolers while being directly responsible for them at all times.

My group support worker, Myra, could easily have passed for an American basketball player. So when in her introductions she said she was once a victim of domestic violence, I was thinking 'How could that have been?'

As if reading my thoughts, she went on to explain that after a six-month courtship, she'd married a man who suffered from 'small man syndrome' and that he'd spent the next 10 years of their lives together trying to 'cut her down to size'. And that he succeeded largely because she didn't know what she was up against. And also because she couldn't believe what she was seeing and hearing from the person she thought she knew differently, so she tried to find explanations for his behaviour...

"So, before I go into the signs of a potentially abusive partner or the early signs of an abusive relationship, I will mention three effects abuse has on its victim: 1) Confusion..." My ears stayed pricked as she continued, "If you can't say for sure whether or not you are in an abusive relationship, you most probably are in one."

The other two kind of washed over me as I chewed on what I'd just heard. Could this be true? Always true? Like gravity?... Myra's words soon come back into focus, "Now feel free to share as much or as little as you are comfortable with..." And so it was introductions and so on and so forth.

And that's been the pattern largely – a little insight into the world of abuse, abusers and victims and little chit-chats amongst group members. Sometimes, though, if somebody had had a particularly bad week and wanted to share, we all rallied round her. No one was allowed to tell anyone else what to do or not to do in their individual situations. Myra would say, "We are about raising awareness, sharing strategies for keeping safe and growing strong; we are a 'support' network, not a 'control' network." She insisted, "Each must be free to do and be whatever they are comfortable with, including stopping sessions whenever they please."

I found the sessions stimulating. I still wasn't sure where I was in relation to being a victim of domestic violence. Some of the symptoms shown by victims of DV also occurred in depression, and I know I have a melancholic outlook and disposition. I was always a sensitive one. But then, as I thought about Ash's relationship with Nathan, I wondered if Nathan didn't have the tendencies I was learning are common to controllers who tend to end up abusing their partners.

And, frankly, it felt good to be in the midst of other adults as I'd given up the luxury of a regular job.

What I found difficult to the point of near distress was assessing Theo against what I was learning to be the 'profile of the controlling partner'. Surely what we were having were communication issues and/or immaturity on his part? I found myself excusing him in my mind, rationalising his behaviour. It wasn't until much later that I realised there was a technical term for that: I was in *denial*.

Summer 2004
Ashleigh (aged 15)

Nathan. This is why I love him:

1. Oh my gosh! I could never guess what he was going to give me next, or when or where. In the last year I've received random gifts like a Japanese fan; a set of Russian dolls stacked into one another; a silver wristwatch (for my last birthday); a 12-carat gold necklace with a forever friends locket (for Christmas); a smoothie maker; a bouquet of (artificial) lilies (for Valentine's); a photo frame; a silver promise ring; a scarf; a digital camera; and a sleek satin black dress with a red sash – not my style but I wear it for him anyway.

2. He is so handsome, sometimes I pinch myself that he chose me to be his girlfriend. I am indeed the envy of all my mates.

3. His voice. He could soothe me to sleep with the same vocal chords that he'd use to break up a gang fight.

4. He respects my wish to wait awhile before getting physically intimate.

And this is why I sometimes wonder about him:

1. He can have any girl he wants, yet he seems terrified of losing me. For example, at a club once *(don't tell Mum!),* I danced with one of Josh's friends while Nathan was taking his time coming back from the

bar. He came right between us, taking me by the hand and shoving Sam with the other, snarling, "Lay off my woman!"

I didn't like the way he behaved. To be honest, it scared me a little bit. But he said it's because he loves me too much. I've never danced with anyone else since then.

2. Sometimes when he kisses certain girls goodbye, it looks too close, much more than a peck and I'm sure I've even seen him brush a boob or two in the course of hanging out with other friends, and sometimes casually grazing his hands against their moons. He says I'm moaning if I ask him about it and that I'm jealous and possessive and that he has eyes and hands only for me, and was willing to wait for me and that I needed to trust him more. And I'm too embarrassed to talk about this with anyone, even though it worries me sometimes. Maybe if I agreed to make out more with him he might not stray with them? I really worry though that making out might lead to putting out and I really am not ready for that. Does that make me a freak?

3. He wants to know what I am thinking all the time. And if I don't feel like sharing, he says I'm shutting him out. Although I'm not. It's just that sometimes I want to be by myself. I just want some space to breathe. Nathan often seems to want to crowd me out.

This confuses me. I really love him, and would like

to spend the rest of my life with him. And he says he loves me, he wants to spend the rest of his life with me, and he showers me with presents whether an occasion calls for it or not. He wouldn't tell me how he could afford these though, but I know his parents are well loaded, so I believe he is clean.

But, like Aunty Beauty says, the rest of my life is a long time, and I need to be sure…

Yet how can I be sure? Mum seems to think that he's my 'Mr Right'. Well, what do you expect – she has a pin-up of Zac Efron in her bedroom.

I don't see much of Josh these days – and to be fair, he doesn't see much of me – so I don't know what he really thinks.

Aunty Daisy says I'm still young and I don't have to commit just yet, and to "trust your guts". Not much use as my guts are in a twist.

I just don't know. I even found myself praying the other day. I said under my breath, "God, I'm confused. I know I don't come to you often, but please help me. My mum says that you hear and answer prayers. If so, please show me a sign of what I should do about Nathan – should I stay with him, or should I break it off?"

This Saturday morning, I updated my Facebook status: 'Fed up browsing Facebook. Don't feel like homework. Guess what? Will go tidy up my bedroom ☺!'

I thought I'd start by cheering myself up – looking through last year's Christmas cards that I still had in a pile on my desk. There was one from Josh: 'To the best sister in whole wide world including the web'. I smile as I remember how that had made me laugh. I do miss Josh. Thank God for Facebook, we remain in each other's world.

Mum's was a regular 'from mum to daughter' card.

Nathan's was: 'To My One and Only Everlasting Love at Christmas and Forever'.

Aunty Beauty's was: 'Merry Christmas Dear One', on a photo of us both taken a few years ago when we all went to Disneyland Paris, and me and Aunty Beauty sat next to each other on the Big Mountain Thrill. You should see the look on our faces. There is no way this is going in the recycling bin.

Inside the card she wrote by hand: 'Dearest Ash, you are precious to me, my very dear niece. And I love you like you were my own daughter. Wishing you a merry Christmas and a happy New Year. Go forth into the New Year, be bold, be brave and pursue your dreams! With love always, Aunty Beauty & Uncle Theo xxx'.

Aunty Beauty. She's so lovely. She looks so sad these days. I wonder if it has to do with her not yet having children of her own? Or Uncle Theo's ridiculous working hours? (I'm slightly scared of him and I don't know why.) She talks with me about real life stuff more than Mum ever does.

I remember one day she came in as Nathan was leaving. After he'd gone, she'd said to me with a twinkle in her eyes, "Do I hear wedding bells any time soon?"

"Not with my consent," Mum chirped from the kitchen, "she's got to complete her education first, and not get interrupted like I was."

"You could still have gone back, you know," Aunty Beauty threw back to Mum. Then she asked me to sit next to her. "So tell me, really, how is it going?"

"Well, so-so. To be honest, sometimes I'm sure, sometimes I'm not. There are times I think I understand him.

There are times when I think I have no clue about him… but I love him, and I know he loves me… so…" I finish with a shrug.

"Darling Ash, you are too young to go into a long-term relationship on a 50% assurance. Let me give you some tips."

She asked me to get my diary/organiser and take notes. I love my Aunty Beauty and her chief librarian ways. But sometimes, like that day, I found it tedious. I was like, "Do I have to?"

My whining voice didn't work on this occasion. She said, "You don't have to, but if you have them down somewhere, you can refer to them if you ever need to, or pass them on to somebody else."

I groaned, "Does it have to be like right now?"

"Nothing like the present moment, my dear," she insisted. Oh Aunty Beauty.

Seeing she wasn't going to give in, I thought I might as well humour her and get it over with, so I got my Betty Boop organiser that, incidentally, was a present from her, and took down her pearls of wisdom. I suddenly had an urgent need to revisit that list today before getting on with the cleaning.

As I haven't used that organiser in a while, I had to ferret through some stuff in my drawers to find it. I turned to the entry which I'd titled 'Aunty Daisy's Recipe for Relationship Bliss – Session 1'.

1) *When in doubt, opt out.*

2) *If you feel disrespected, you are being disrespected – don't argue yourself out of it.*

3) *Self-preservation is the first rule of survival. If you feel unsafe with him, then you are unsafe with him. Don't try to reason it out. Allow yourself to act in your own best interests – this is not being selfish, it is being wise.*

4) *Trust your instincts more than you trust him.*

5) *If you feel intimidated by him, then you are being intimidated by him.*

6) *If his words of love and his actions don't add up, believe his actions over his words.*

7) *Love is gracious.*

8) *Love is kind.*

9) *Love is peaceful, peaceable and pure.*

10) *Love empowers, it doesn't paralyse.*

11) *Love frees, it never imprisons.*

12) *Love gives, it never drains.*

Be aware. Let your head work with your heart as you navigate these waters.

I trust you to look after yourself. Go ahead and do just that.

When I came to the end of the entry, I was like Oh my gosh, is this a sign? If so, what does it mean for me? Oh help!!

Summer 2004
Theo

She doesn't look at me the way she used to – as a matter of fact, she hardly looks at me at all. And when she does, there is something I can't quite place – I used to be able to read her like a book. My Beauty – I wish she would relax with me again.

I decided to raise my concerns the other Sunday after a leisurely lie-in (she goes to church more these days, but only when I'm on duty). Putting on my sombre monotone, I said, "I think there's something not quite right."

"What is it?" She looked like a little frightened kitten in her black and white flannel bathrobe.

"Us." Pause. "There is something not quite right about us."

She shuffles on the bed and still says nothing.

"What do you think?"

"I think," her tone was measured, "you are beginning to wake up to smell the coffee."

"And you say that because…?"

"Because when I've tried to speak with you about it in the past, you've always swept it under the carpet. You tell me to be strong. To be like this or that or the other person. So what do you expect?"

To be frank, I was quite surprised to see her get stirred up like that. This is usually the kind of conversation that would ordinarily melt her little yellow vanilla-flavoured heart. I hadn't prepared for this, so naturally I went into my 'attack is the best form of defence' mode.

"So you are saying it's my fault?"

"Well, a lot of it is."

"And the part that isn't?"

"It's the part where I've allowed you to run roughshod over me."

"Beauty! You are out of your mind!"

She rolled over and got off the bed. Took a few deliberate steps to my side of it and sat down beside me, looking me fully in the eyes. I will never forget the defiance I saw. I will never forget the tone of her voice when she said, "You are out of order for yelling at me. That is abuse, and I will no longer stand for it."

I grabbed her arm as she made to walk away. "You dare accuse me of abusing you? I've never laid a hand on you."

"And that makes it all right? Let go of me."

I didn't. Not at first. I needed to know what was happening to my wife. "What has got into you?" I tried to keep my voice firm and controlled. I'm not quite sure that it worked, which simply increased my levels of anxiety. Now she's accusing me of abuse... unbelievable!

"Theo, you are hurting me. And you have right now perjured your own testimony, for you are squeezing the very life out of my arm."

I released my grip almost involuntarily. "I'm sorry, Beauty, I didn't mean to hurt you."

"You always say that, but is it really true? Think about it."

Within a few minutes, she was showered and dressed. And said she was going shopping.

She didn't return till close to midnight. Her words haunted me all through those hours she was away. And I deeply regretted having held her that tightly – I'd forgotten my own strength and I knew that my fingerprints would remain tattooed on her delicate skin for a very long time.

We didn't speak for days. Which was very unlike Beauty – she couldn't stand to receive or even to give the silent treatment. Now though, she spoke to me only when it was essential. She turned her back on me when she was in bed. And all my jokes that used to get me out of sticky situations fell on stony ground. I had to devise a plan to break the ice and have my beautiful wife back in my bosom where she belonged.

Flowers. Why didn't I think of that earlier? To make it extra special, I arranged to have them delivered to the house during the day. It would be a surprise as it wasn't her birthday, or Valentine's or any special day. I asked the florist at Stratford station to make me a bouquet that would have as dramatic an impact as the falling of the Berlin Wall. The price wasn't a hindrance. And florist Sue let her imagination run riot with a combination of apple blossoms, daffodils, some sparkle-treated twigs with curly tips, some lilies and one single red rose. She took her time to educate me on the significance of each item, but all I wanted was for Beauty to see that I was sorry.

On the card, I wrote by hand: '*A thing of Beauty is a joy forever. You are my everlasting joy and I love you forever and a day. Love always, Theo.*'

I asked Sue to be sure to deliver it at 12.30. They'd have had their lunch and Sunita would be having her midday nap while Beauty read or pottered round the house or did whatever it was she did with her time. She wasn't one for daytime TV except for what she'd scheduled for Sunita.

I expected my phone to ring any time between half twelve and one. However, when it went off at 12.40 and it was Sue at the other end, it took me a moment to recover from the shock and take in what she was saying.

"What do you mean she's not home? Maybe she's having a nap. Keep your thumb on the doorbell if you have to."

"I did, Theo, but there's been no response, and I've got to get back to the stall."

"She's got to be home – is there a VW Golf in the driveway?"

"No, there's no car at all."

"Is there one in the neighbour's drive? The number 21 neighbour is usually home."

"Yes, there is."

"Okay, leave it with Mrs Khan, and a note for Beauty to pick it up when she comes in."

It wasn't until I called her mobile phone and it kept going to voicemail that I began to panic. An hour or so later, I asked to take the rest of the day off due to a personal emergency.

The home looked normal when I got in, so she couldn't have run away. I'm her next of kin so I'd have heard by now if there'd been any accidents. Or incidents. For the next 60 minutes or so, I crawled round the usual places Beauty visited. I didn't want to call any family or friend. I needed to know first and deal with the situation. It's too soon to report them as missing persons, but in the end I decided to go back to the office so I could monitor communications in case any report/information came in from or about her.

When I saw her face flashing on my mobile phone, I was surprised at the number of knots that began to loosen around my temples and my neck. She sounded so normal on the phone. She'd seen my missed calls, she said; why hadn't I left a message? she queried.

"Where were you?" was all I could manage without exploding.

"I took Sunita for a spin."

"I see. You home now?"

"Yes we are. So, what's up, why did you call?"

"I missed you, and just wanted to hear your voice."

The rest of the day was grey. I stayed away until I knew Sunita would have been picked up. I needed to find out where Beauty was. I always knew her whereabouts – well, almost always. This is the second time she's made me panic by disappearing without communicating with me, and making it impossible for me to reach her on the phone. And this will be the last, I will be sure of it.

The flowers were sitting regally in the middle of the dining table. I could smell dinner, and could sense Beauty was in a glorious mood. Well, I wasn't.

I returned her 'welcome home' kiss with stoic silence. I turned off the music, turned on the TV, flopped on my special chair and threw my legs on the coffee table.

"For someone who seemed desperate to hear my voice earlier, you seem a bit withdrawn. Did something happen at work?"

After an appropriate pause, I replied, "Work was fine. Until you went missing."

"Me? I didn't go missing," she chuckled. "Who reported me missing?"

"The florist."

"But she left me a note – thanks for the flowers by the way, they are beautiful. What's the occasion?"

"It doesn't matter. It's been spoilt now."

"How?"

"By your mysterious disappearance."

"Please don't blow this into something else. Can I not go out with Sunita on the fly? Do I have to clear everything with you first?"

"As a matter of fact, yes." I throw my feet on to the floor and get on them in one swift move. I lean towards her. "I need to know where you are to be sure you are all right."

Stepping away slightly, she goes, "Well, you didn't know where I was, but I am all right. So please relax."

"How can I relax when my wife is making a fool of me?"

"I beg your pardon?"

"I've been thinking about it all day. You've been acting strangely lately, and then you go off like that – I'm pretty certain you are seeing somebody."

"I don't believe you are accusing me of cheating on you!" She was shaking her head and turning away from me.

"Aren't you? Look me in the eye and tell me you're not."

She looked at me squarely and said, "I will not dignify that question with an answer." Then she made to turn towards the kitchen, but I'd swiftly stepped in her path, careful not to restrain her with my hands.

"Excuse me please, I have things to do."

"You go nowhere, you do nothing until you tell me where you were this afternoon."

"And if I don't?"

"Then it's true. You are a filthy little cheat, an *ashawo*. Prove me wrong."

She was silent, for what seemed for ever. When she

spoke, her words were laced with such anger and resentment that I felt ashamed, an emotion I don't often indulge in. This feeling soon passed as I heard more of what she was saying.

"… I went to a support group for women in abusive relationships… whatever doubts I had about whether you were indeed being abusive, you have kindly clarified. Now if you will excuse me."

Involuntarily, I made way for her. I immediately regretted this – I am losing her, this was unacceptable. I don't know why I did it but I flung the flower vase with its contents against the wall. And I don't know how it happened but my knuckles were bleeding and swollen. I saw I was sweating profusely and cursing generously. I knew I was out of line, but I was too stressed out to do anything about it.

Eventually I calmed myself down and decided to try again, a softer approach this time. When I got to the bedroom door, the little toe-rag had locked it.

I'm sorry to report that I threatened to kick it in. She dared me to do it and promised to report me to the police if I did. That was when it clicked. What was I doing? I was supposed to be protecting her, reassuring her. The idea of the flowers was to surprise her with an elaborate apology. How did I let it all get so out of hand?

"I'm very sorry, Beauty, I don't know what came over me. I was so afraid that I'd lost you, that you didn't love me anymore."

Silence. Intense and deafening.

"Oh Beauty. Oh my Beauty. I'm extremely sorry. I love you too much. You're the best thing that's happened to me. I can't live without you. If I hurt you, I will only be hurting myself. And you can't live without me either, can you? Let's stop rowing. Let's rekindle our flame and enjoy our lives together. I promise never again to hurt you with my actions, or with my words. I am very sorry."

Eventually, having run out of words, I crumpled to the floor of the bedroom door and simply sobbed.

Two or three hours later, I was back in bed, with a blotched-faced Beauty, folded foetus-like within my arms. I go off to sleep with a calm assurance that everything will be all right after all.

CHAPTER 12

Early 2006
Beauty

I know how my heart thumps with every tread of his steps. Sometimes I sense him before I see him, the shiver scurrying down my spine before I hear him. Still, I'm startled at the sound of my name carried by his voice.

I love Theo. That's my problem. I stopped attending the AADV + VA support group as it made him so very sad. I thought I'd be okay. And I have been, we have been… but for the dreams.

Many times I've wondered how life would be for me without Theo. I seem to find the answer in the dream where it's chucking it down with rain and, at the same time, brownish leaves are being swirled all around me where I sat as I was – fat, old and alone on a bench. Sometimes it's a bench in a park. Sometimes it's a bench at a bus stop. At other times it's been at a train station, and just once so far, it's been the churchyard at St Katherine's where my three little babies lie.

The other night, I woke up sweating all over and with a sensation of swelling in my throat. In the dream, Theo and I had gone to church to renew our vows. I wasn't too keen on it at first. I thought that having been married for x number of years we could just renew our vows to each other by living them daily. But Theo was adamant that as a sign that the war between us was well and truly over, it would be a good idea to mark our 'new life' together under the canopy of God's blessings and in the presence of family and friends who, I must say, were all sold on the idea.

"That's great," was Daisy's verdict, "whatever doubts you may have had about his love for you can now be laid to rest."

And Mel was, "Wao! You get to marry the same guy twice! Surely, that must make it last forever."

It was such a vivid one, this dream. I remember saying to her, "Why don't I feel excited about it then? What if, in fact, I can't bear for it to last forever?"

"Come on, B, this is the well-known pre-wedding nerves."

"Mel, you are not listening to me. We are not engaged. We are already married. If this is what forever will be, then..." I choked up.

"Okay, Beauty, I can hear you. What if you saw it as a promise of a better tomorrow?"

"That could work," I nodded, while willing back my tears.

"And you get an opportunity to dress up again in your pretty princess wedding dress."

"Oh no! That won't fit. Not even if I lived on air for the next six weeks!"

Anyway, as is usually the way with dreams, some of the finer details were non-existent when I awoke. Like where exactly did it take place? Who was the officiating minister? And most importantly, what exactly did we promise each other?

I thought it funny though that my dress was an almost exact replica of my real wedding dress, but two sizes larger, and calf-length without a train, unlike the real one. And of course Sunita was my little flower girl who walked before me down the aisle towards Theo who was resplendent in his formal officer dress – very different from the tux he'd hired for the real wedding.

At the end of the ceremony when all the photoshoots had been done, drinks and cakes drunk and eaten and everyone else was gone, Theo and I thought to make the most of the glorious weather and take a walk in the park before going home. As soon as we got there, it began to rain, lightly at first then soon heavily enough for puddles to form and splash on my lovely ivory lightly sequinned dress. I started to cry and turned to Theo saying, "My dress is all messed up," but he wasn't there. I began to call out to him frantically, in the rain, searching for him in Victoria Park, and woke up with his name on my lips and a lump in my throat.

This certainly competes with last night's for the 'weirdest dreams of the month' Oscar awards.

I was sitting at the foot of Nelson's Column in Trafalgar Square, as if stuck to it by bird poop. Neither rain nor wind nor leaves could move me. It was the fattest I've ever seen myself even in my dreams. I heard a baby cry, then I turned around to follow the sound. Next thing I knew, I was in St James's Park with Theo, sitting beside him on a bench, holding this baby. I tried to have a conversation with Theo, but he never responded. Eventually, he turned in our direction and said to the baby, "Hello little one! How did you get here? Are you lost? Let's go find your parents." Then he made to pick up the baby and I woke up screaming, "No! No! No!" my bed soaked with my sweat…

This might be a good time to go see a therapist.

Sunita is still my only ward. I've loved having her as a part of my life. It doesn't feel like a job at all. However, my time with her is now very short. As she's now three and a half, she's started going part-time to preschool. Daisy still drops her off to me at 8am and picks her up at six. I do the school runs and miss her dreadfully those two and a half hours when she's away. What will I do when she starts full time in September?

Theo seems to be getting warmer towards the adoption idea – at least we talk about it now, unlike before. I understand it being difficult for him – he is a very responsible person and cannot understand why people will shirk their responsibilities and get away with it. By adopting, he feels we would be helping some irresponsible adult get away with shirking.

"But what about the child?" I asked. "Should they have to suffer continually?"

"No, the child shouldn't, but by making it easy for them, more mothers will continue to walk away."

"What about the fathers?"

"It's more of a mother thing."

"Yes, but if some of the mothers were more supported, probably they would feel more able to keep the baby."

"Yeah, true. However, a mother shouldn't be able to give up her baby so easily."

"Who said it was easy?"

"How do you know it's not? Have you given up one?"

"How do you know it's easy? Have you given up one?" I return his question to him.

And that was the easiest conversation we've had on the topic. I am open to adopting a child of any race, colour or creed. The younger, the better. Theo wouldn't want anyone under five years old (too demanding); doesn't want a boy (only his biological son should bear his name); and the child has to be black (not even mixed race) – and that simply doesn't make sense to me as our biological children would have been mixed race.

Being so tired, as was often the case with me these days, I decided that this was a conversation to leave for another day. Meanwhile, the nightly visions will not go away...

Early 2006
Ashleigh (aged 16)

I still can't believe Nathan.

It all started during my 16th birthday last August. I had plans for my day, you know? I wanted a cosy dinner with family and close friends. I had one of two places in mind. Eventually I decided on *The Harvester's* because of the huge variety of its menu, the fact that it wasn't too far to get to, and the semi-formal nature of its happy-go-lucky set up. To be sure we could all be accommodated, I made a reservation. I'd told everyone to clear their diaries and be ready with their credit cards so all I needed to do was inform them of the precise place and the precise time.

Nathan was to pick me from home at about 5pm so we could have some special time together before joining the others at 7.30pm. It was a surprise treat from him and he wouldn't even give a hint at what it was. Well, I was happy to wait – I loved surprises.

When I heard my bedroom door creaking open that afternoon at about half three, I thought Mum had finished work early. I kept my eyes fixed on the mirror, intent on finishing off that last stroke of eyeliner as I said, "You're back early."

"Happy birthday, Ash." I dropped my eye pencil at the sound of the muffled voice, swinging my chair in its direction. I only had a fraction of a minute to take in the two balaclava-clad figures before they were by my side.

The speaker carried on, "Sorry we have to do this, but we are under instructions."

"Excuse me? Who are you and what do you want?" I tried to keep the panic out of my voice as scenes from various episodes of *Law and Order* flashed through my mind.

"To accompany you for the rest of the evening for your birthday surprise," he said, placing the Minnie Mouse patterned blindfold tenderly but firmly over my eyes and tying it up behind my head, messing up my delicate up-do in the process – all those hours in the salon going down the drain, and without a chance to put on my tiara.

"Just so you know, my uncle is a cop. You will not get away with this."

It was the last thing I said before he tied the lavender-scented scarf around my nose and mouth, a bit tighter than necessary, I thought. As if reading my thoughts, one of them adjusted it a tad, giving me room to breathe. Obviously they didn't want me dead – at least not straightaway.

"Now, be a good girl, do as you are told and no one gets hurt," Muffler continued. "Each of us will take one of your hands, we will take you to a vehicle, and drive you to your destination."

My destination? I shook my head furiously. They each took my hand in their gloved ones anyway and guided me through the flat, down the stairs, into a revving car in the parking lot. As we walked silently, I could perceive a faintly familiar smell, but couldn't quite place it.

They sat on either side of me after doing up my seat belt and off we went to I don't know where.

My mind went into overdrive. What will Nathan do when he gets to me and I'm not there? I don't even have my mobile phone on me.

What about Mum? If I don't turn up at the restaurant at half seven, will she put it down to my usual tardiness? At what point will she begin to worry? What then? Will Uncle Theo jump straight into a rescue mission? When will I officially be declared missing? Will I still be alive anyway? What if they thought I ran away – then they might not suspect foul play… Oh my gosh, and I have been threatening to run away from home for so long!

What do these people want? It can't be money – how much can they expect to get from a single parent who lives in a council flat? It can't be… no, I've got to think of positive things else I'd be gone before they even get me to the destination. To die on my 16th birthday never featured in any of my plans, including the running away from home ones. One way or another, it's looking like these are my final moments on the earth.

Somehow, accepting that this was the end seemed to have helped; I was surprised to find myself nodding off to sleep. The radio was now a soothing lullaby, my captors now my bodyguards…

I awoke in a bed, with Nathan on a chair beside me, a frown framing his perfect face which relaxed into a smile as he saw me stir. "Hey babe, are you okay? You gave me a fright there for a minute."

"My head is splitting. I am woozy. Where am I? And how did you find me?"

"You are at the top of *Club Rocky* where your 16th birthday party is in full swing at the moment."

It was then I decided I was still asleep. This wasn't my room. And my birthday party was at *The Harvester's* where right now my mum must be going spare with worry.

"Come on babe, I know the journey was a surprise and the guys had to gag you for everyone's safety. But you're here and well, so please get up, get dressed, let's rock and roll."

His words were coming to me from very far away. His lips were moving out of sync with what he was saying. And it took me a while to begin to take it all in. I gradually pulled myself into a sitting position so I could look directly across at Nathan.

"You mean I am awake?"

"Of course you are!"

"And I am alive and well?"

"Yes, I can pinch you if you want." And he did actually pinch me before I could decide whether I wanted him to do so or not.

"So, why am I here? And what's been going on?" I was struggling to keep my voice firm.

Nathan stroking my cheeks, was like, "It's okay baby, I arranged a surprise party for you."

"But I told you I didn't want a big party?"

"I know, hence I had to do it this way and get the guys to come for you."

I slowly got on my feet, hands on my hips, drew close to him. "You kidnap me to get me to a party for me? How messed up is that? What if I'd been hurt?"

"It's crazy only because I love you so much and couldn't let a milestone birthday like this go without a bang."

"It's **my** birthday. It wasn't going without a bang, I had it all planned, and my mum, she'll be out of her mind with worry. You have no right… "

"Oh don't worry about her or any of your family members – they know you are with me."

I felt my knees wobble and had to hold on to the bed frame for support. "You told them you were kidnapping me to a surprise party?"

He sniggered, "Don't be silly, only that I'd arranged something else for you today – to which they are welcome."

"Will they be coming then?"

"Not a chance – oldies don't turn up at places like this – but I have reserved a decent table for them should they decide to grace the occasion. But I'm pretty sure Josh will be here, and if you don't turn up shortly, he's going to be coming for my head."

That was some six months ago. It was the most awful day of my life. Nathan introduced me to this crowd of screaming, burping and bopping strangers as his 'woman'. He told me how happy he was that I was now a woman. And that legally I could pretty much do whatever I chose with him. As the night wore on, he got weirder and weirder and he couldn't seem to keep his hands or his mouth off me.

By 10pm, with half the crowd being tipsy and leery, I told Nathan I was ready to go home. "It's not yet midnight, Cinderella. Just a couple more hours and I'll let you off while the rest of us proper adults rock the night away."

I had to raise my voice above the din, "Nathan, take me home! Now!"

"And if I don't?"

"Well then, I'll walk." As I made to walk past him, he grabbed my hand, laughing, "Do you even know how far you are from the nearest bus stop?"

"But I do." Oh thank you Josh, I mouthed to him.

"Come on Ash, let's get the heck out of this place."

Early 2006
Melody

The light has gone out of her eyes. I know she hasn't stopped crying; yet she doesn't need to cry – he was a jerk and she's well rid of him.

I should have seen it coming. I should have taken better care of my baby. I should have listened more to Beauty's reservations about Nathan and I most certainly should not have agreed to his surprise party nonsense. I am only grateful to God that she wasn't physically hurt. The effects of the sleeper she'd inhaled have long since worn off. As for the emotional wounds, worsened by his lies about her on Facebook, I can only pray for divine healing for her, and mercy for me. For I have failed my daughter. Again. I didn't protect her. If I'd given her a father, perhaps he could have protected her better. Even though her dad didn't stay, I was young, I could have met and married somebody else and raised both of them in a 'proper' family.

But I'm hopeful. She hasn't given up her dreams of going to university to study to be a teacher. And Josh, he's been such an encouragement to all of us, evidence that God does answer prayers; that there is always hope; that things can indeed get better. And I have to deliberately remember this rather frequently these days.

Josh is only home some holidays now, and even when he's here, he's different, grown up like. Ash's leaving home soon. What will I do with myself then?

When Beauty and I ran away from home in Warri all those years ago, I never thought I would one day miss 'home'. And I didn't – until recently. When I look in the mirror these days, I see staring back at me a lighter skinned version of my Aunty Mary. I must look to my kids the way she looked to me when I was a teenager. But she was wiser, that's the difference. And though she was single all her life and had no children of her own, her life was full and purposeful. She wasn't stuck behind some counter as a 'checkout girl'. Mind you, this job has paid the bills all these years. But my heart has never been in it, maybe now is the time to locate my heart and follow it.

What, though, if it leads me back home? Will I have the wherewithal to follow it? Do I really want to? Dad is dead. Aunt Mary is old. I have no real relationship with my half-sisters and stepmother. All my life really is here.

But… I remember how it was there, then. You never grew old and died alone (except if they thought you were a witch or something, then you were roundly ostracised).

You never had to pull the grey hairs out of your head all by yourself (but then a mischievous cousin could pull the black ones as well, leaving you with bald patches in addition to severe pain).

You never had to talk audibly to yourself to be sure your voice was still working.

You were certainly never overshadowed by the sounds of silence.

I probably would have been a social outcast anyway

– a single parent whose children did not know their father? What a scandal. A body of attitude that presumes the woman guilty at the slightest hint of a relationship breakdown would not have worked to my advantage. But perhaps it would have compelled me to work harder at my relationships. Probably my children would each have known their dad, or at least the truth about them.

What a freak of nature I am, belonging neither here nor there. And how can I take this with me to my grave? Will it be fair, will it be right? What can I do to make it all right?

Discretion is the better part of valour
Honesty is the best policy
There is sorrow in too much knowledge
Deception is a cruel act

What do I do? Which of these apply to me?

"My Lord, my God, help me take the right path. Show me which way to go. Give me a fresh revelation of your love for me, in spite of my past errors and present doubts, help me to hide myself under the shadow of your wings. Help me to be still and to know that you are God… and that you will cause everything to work out right, because I love you, and I believe you have called me according to your purpose… Amen."

CHAPTER 13

23rd June, 2006. Theo's 40th birthday
Theo

One of the reasons I was attracted to the police force above the other uniformed professions is the order it brings into the everyday life of its community. It brings my love for order and for community into one sphere, feeds my need for structure and the security that a level of certainty brings with it. The uncertainties inherent in the job add the spice that expels the gremlins of boredom, for boredom feeds rebellion and rebellion brings anarchy.

I smiled as I reread the last bit. I wasn't too keen initially when I was told that I was to visit one of the local school's careers days and speak about a career in the police force. Then after I agreed to do it (I didn't have much of a choice really), I struggled over what to say. One evening as I sat glued to the TV but not seeing, pen and pad in hand but not writing, Beauty asked if she could help.

"Frankly, this is more up your street. What do I say to a bunch of teenagers about the police force?"

"Do you love working there?"

"Of course! Is that a question?"

"Hey! If you're going to be like that – do it your own way!"

"I'm sorry, sweetie, I didn't mean to snap."

"Why the police force? Why not say the army or navy or air force?"

Then I saw what she was doing. By the end of the

exercise, we had drafted a little speech that showed a part of me I would not ordinarily reveal. But Beauty's point was that the kids needed to know that there is a heart in the force, and what better way to show this than to open up what it means to me personally and how it affects the community globally.

The speech went so well, many kids requested further information and a couple of the girls even asked for an autograph! For the first time in my life, I was close to being a celebrity. And it was all thanks to Beauty.

My dear brainy Beauty. I sometimes wonder if the 'gremlins of boredom' are getting to her. I think now that maybe I shouldn't have encouraged her to go on that blasted *Early Years* course. Since that course, she seems to have lost all sense of purpose and perspective. Subsequently, she seems to be looking for one cause or another to champion; she's now getting about as cantankerous as the slightly off-balanced elderly Mrs Smith down at Tentercourt Place whose neighbours are on the phone to us at least once a week to settle one matter or the other.

Take my 40th for example. It's my birthday after all and I should have a say – well, and my way – about how it should be celebrated. So I wanted a cruise – not just because I've wanted one for years, but also because it would be an opportunity for us to spend the elusive 'quality time' together, only this time it would also be in quantity – two full weeks without interruption from work or any other aspects of our lives at home, to explore new places and new experiences together. I thought it would reignite our romance, and bridge the gulf that seems to be increasingly edging its way between us.

My time off work was already settled. I'd researched

a few places, but frankly, I wouldn't have minded which of the cruises as long as I was aboard with the love of my life. So I gave her the first option – Mediterranean or Caribbean? Surely she couldn't now accuse me of taking unilateral decisions, something she's been doing a lot of herself lately.

"Neither," was all she offered. I sat at the end of dinner, waiting for an elaboration. When none was forthcoming, I said, "Why neither – do you want to go on a different cruise?"

"No, Theo, I don't want to go on a cruise at all."

"But it's my birthday and I want to go on a cruise with you. Is that too much to ask?"

"No, it's not. But look at it this way. You are 40 only once. Would it not be better to mark it with family and friends rather than with strangers on the ocean somewhere?"

"But I'll be with you."

"Yes, I know, but if you did it here, you'll also be with me."

The sadness in her eyes mitigated my rising rage. I had to fight to not be overwhelmed by my deflation. "So what do you suggest?"

"Well, we could have friends and family over for dinner or go out to a restaurant or something… we could always do the cruise another time."

So that was how my birthday cruise sank faster than the Titanic.

And D-Day is here. At home, the dinner party organised by Beauty will be kicking off in another couple of hours or so. I must say though that she has thrown herself into it, dragging me along with such a determination and enthusiasm that I soon lost my grumpy reluctance along the way.

The first major hurdle was deciding between a formal sit-down dinner and a buffet. Once we'd agreed on the buffet style, we arranged the lounge in a rough triangle. The side nearest the kitchen had the largest table. This would hold the food. Then there was a round table that held the well-labelled drinks: ginger beer, lemonade, buoy shot (a cocktail of Captain Morgan, orange juice and a touch of cherry); buoy coke (Captain Morgan and Coca-Cola) and ahoy! (Mt Gay rum with a dash of sherry and some cinnamon spice).

I was a bit concerned with having so much alcoholic drink available while we had youngsters on our guest list. But Beauty allayed my fears, reminding me that Ash was teetotaller and Josh had grown to be a responsible young man who could be trusted. Sunita – well, she was just too little to be able to help herself to drinks.

And the third angle had the other round table which just about fitted nine standard chairs and one high one. As I put the finishing touches to the décor – navy and white broad-striped tablecloths with mini sailboats dotted over them, placing matching serviettes in strategic locations and a touch of blue and silver glitter here and there – my mind drifted to some of our expected guests.

Simon and Sandra. They bring a kind of spark to every setting that is uniquely theirs. She has a way with words, doesn't say a lot, but what she does say is usually packed. Simon does more of the talking, and from what he says, they are missing the twins a lot and can't wait for the grandchildren to start popping out so they can get busy with grandparenting.

Rob. He has done well holding the fort – both business and home – while Daisy recovered from her depression. I don't quite understand it – how a perfectly healthy and happy lady who wanted a baby could suffer from depression on having a fulfilment of her heart's desire. But then, I'm neither a doctor nor a psychologist and I am intrigued by the complexities of human nature, especially of the female variety.

Joshua. He seems to have settled down a lot. He's completed his diploma and is hoping to go to university in the autumn. I couldn't help smiling as I recalled the flak I received from Beauty and Mel following the detention incident. But here he is, a living example to the testimony that sometimes extreme measures are required in desperate situations. And the way he stood up for Ash and rescued her from her thug of a boyfriend at that party last year – what a gentleman.

Poor Ash, she seems to be still broken over Nathan – not that she speaks much to me, but I can sense it, and it sometimes gets my goat that I didn't do something to rattle that S O B who would dare kidnap my niece in the name of a party. I think I let her down there. I believe I did.

Actually, I may have let her down well before now. I still wonder sometimes what it would have been like if I'd gone with Mel instead. But she was already a mum, you see, and I didn't think it right that I should father another's child. Plus she wasn't completely free of him anyway, and by the time she was well and truly free, she was a mother of two.

I thought it best to start from scratch with Beauty. Which is ironical as now we are talking about adoption and ultimately me having to father another's child (or children, as Beauty is so besotted with the idea of having many).

Still, I made my bed, I lie on it... that was my last

thought till Beauty, looking gorgeous in her blue, white, yellow and red African print halter-neck maxi dress was stirring me gently. "Wake up Theo, our first guests have arrived."

23rd June, 2006. Theo's 40th birthday
Melody

They bless my heart, my two children – I beg your pardon, young adults. Flanking me on either side were Josh to my left, hair unplaited in honour of Theo who can't stand boys' hair in braids, and Ash to my right, resplendent in her spaghetti-strapped evening dress, looking every bit like Beauty did as a teenager. She seems to be getting over Nathan now, and looking forward to college in September. I am looking forward to a bright future for her of course, but now wasn't the time to dwell on the implications of that for me, so I must deliberately move my mind to thinking of something else, something inspiring, something worthy of my mental energy… like for instance, she is going to college from home, unlike Josh who thought it best to move away and start afresh in Hull.

Because she considered the catfish *peppersoup* to be a bit on the spicy side (it was mild for me though), Beauty thought it would be best if we all sat down to have that. "Thereafter," she'd said, "everyone can feel free to pick and mix whatever they want whenever and however they want it."

Sitting next to Josh were Sandra and Simon. And beside him was Theo. Next to Ash was Rob, then Sunita, and Daisy who was right next to Beauty. Theo and Beauty were almost directly opposite me. And I could see that she was positively glowing. And Theo, he looked pleased, humming along to the Bob Marley number playing in the background.

I am pleased to see them this way, having overcome the rough patch they had a while ago. This then surely must be a good time to share... or is it?

The *peppersoup* did its job – stimulating my appetite and raising a lot of culinary queries from the other guests. Not wanting to miss out on anything, I had a little bit from each of the other appetisers: angel hair pasta with shrimps and basil, and baked crab, brie with artichoke dip. Considering I don't like cheese, I should've given the latter a miss. I needed another helping of *peppersoup* to bring my taste buds back to base.

By the end of the main course – seafood paella and grilled fish with spicy chips – I was ready to burst. It's not as though I had to have everything; the reason there was more than one dish was so people had a choice, and stuffing oneself wasn't part of the deal, I don't think. I'm usually quite temperate, but today the nerves seem to be getting the better of me... I'd better be careful with the drinks and just stick to lemonade.

It's just as well that there were games planned before we got to the cutting of the liner of a cake. As if she read my thoughts, Beauty announced, "It's time for some party games. First it's musical statues to burn off some calories before we light Theo's 40 candles. Sunita and I will be the judges."

"Before then, I have something to say," said Theo as he got up, gesticulating with the long glass he was sipping from. "I want to say thank you to everyone."

"It's not yet time for a vote of thanks, love," Beauty's protest fell on deaf ears.

"Thank you for taking the time to come to this beautiful dinner party organised by my wife. It certainly beats being in her company for two weeks, and apart from the slightly burnt paella and an unduly expensive watch for a present, this is certainly the best birthday I've ever had."

Seeing the colour drain from Beauty, I knew I had to do something.

"So it's hip, hip, hip hurray to the birthday boy," I chimed. Thankfully, everyone joined in:

"Hip, hip, hip, hurray! Hip, hip, hip, hurray! For he's a jolly good fellow, he's a jolly good fellow, for he's a jolly good fellow! And so say all of us, hurray!"

Thereafter it was musical statues (which Ash won), beach blanket bingo (I still don't understand the rules of the game, but Simon won that) and Pictionary (which my group rightfully won). It was cake cutting at 9.15ish and winding down at 10pm. Such a wonderful atmosphere, an excellent party in every way.

But for the fact of it being a Tuesday, it may have carried on till the small hours. I offered to stay behind and help clean up, so Josh took Ash home.

Without speaking, labour was divided into Beauty in the kitchen, me and Theo in the lounge. For some reason, it felt odd being alone with Theo in one room. Willing myself to focus and live in the now, I smiled at him, "Good party unh?"

"Sure. The best. Now I can look forward to the cruise as just a regular holiday."

He didn't seem to be taking much care in taking

down the balloons and lanterns dropping down from the ceiling. Oh well, he might find redecorating therapeutic.

"Well, you can see it as a second honeymoon."

He chuckled, and really looked like he enjoyed the thought. Then I took in what he was saying, "Everything with Beauty is so flabby now, there's no honey left in the moons."

"Have you had too much to drink? Do you realise you are talking about my sister? To me?"

"No, Mel dear, I'm not drunk. And yes, I am talking about your sister. I think I got short-changed."

"What do you mean?"

"I got the wrong sister. It should have been you."

"And when did you determine that?" I was surprised at how angry I got, and how quickly too. But there was no holding back now. "Was it after you went off and left me with child? Or was when you realised you couldn't have one with…"

"Hey! Cool it! You already had a child, remember?"

"Yes, I remember. And there was another one coming when you upped and left me for Beauty." Oh my God, what have I done?

"I beg your pardon?"

"Yes, Ash was on the way."

The longest silence ever.

"You never told me." His voice dripped with – anger? Sadness?

"You'd left by the time I found out. I wouldn't make you break up with Beauty out of some distorted sense of duty to my unborn child. If you loved me, you'd have stayed. And you didn't."

"So, why didn't you tell me?" Okay, it was clearer

now, certainly anger. Very much of it.

"Because it wasn't necessary. You'd left. Nick was trying to get back on the scene. I thought we might work things out. We didn't. He left. You married Beauty… and some 16 years later, here we are…"

Another long pause.

"Look, Theo," I continued as he shrugged my hand off his shoulder, "this isn't how I'd planned to tell you. I am really sorry to shock you like this, but I'm glad it's out. Now I have to come out clean to Ash, and to Josh, and finally to Nick when I do find him, so everyone knows the score."

"What about Beauty?"

"What about her?"

"Who's to tell her? And how can I be sure this is true?"

"I will, but not today, I'll pick the time and place. Just look after her for me, and stop being so insensitive to her. There was no need for those jibes in your supposedly thank you speech, you know that."

"Ash doesn't look like me," his head was shaking, as if of its own accord.

"No, she looks like Beauty. And they get on well, so I guess that helps. If you like, there are tests…"

I didn't see it coming. "You get out of my house and stay out," he roared. "Leave Beauty to me and get out! Now!" His face was suddenly a mask of the *Ewuwu* masquerade. His voice, a combination of a rattlesnake and a bulldog, pierced through my heart into my spine. I suddenly felt like using the bathroom, but didn't dare move…

"Is everything all right?" Beauty ran in from the kitchen, dishcloth in hand, worry written all over her brow. She looked from me to Theo who was back on his easy chair, vigorously working his right leg that's crossed over his left, and then back to me.

"Yes, all is well. I was just leaving. I'll see myself to the door. Thanks for a lovely evening." And I skulked into the night.

23rd June, 2006. Theo's 40th birthday
Beauty

I don't miss him now when he goes away. I'm ashamed to admit it to myself, but I'm actually quite pleased when he is out of town on duty. I feel like a breath of fresh air, a new petal daring to stretch out as spring breaks in.

Sunita broke into my thoughts, "Do you want a bistik, Aunty B?" I scooped her to my bosom, soft Rich Tea and all, and did our special swing-around two step two lunge dance – it always sends Sunita into hysterics, and me along with her. Today though, it helped mask my tears. They've been popping up more frequently now, at the most inopportune times, and in the most inauspicious places I find myself tearful and I don't always know why.

This time though, I knew – Sunita is going into full-time school soon. And yes, I could and will begin to take on other children, but there's a place in my heart reserved only for Sunita. I had considered homeschooling her, but dropped the idea in a hurry. It's not my call, and besides, Theo will certainly have something to say about that.

Anyway, to help me cope with the transition, I've planned so much between now and 2nd September for

Sunita and me to do, my digital camera and camcorder working harder now than ever before. So when Theo came up with his birthday cruise idea, I knew immediately that it wouldn't sail.

And besides, I remember the last time we went away together. We were going through a stormy season (we seem to always be going through those). This was a few weeks after I'd lost Frankie. Theo was always opposed to counselling of any sort, but was happy to flow with the holiday idea. I thought the sea air would do us some good and the sun would certainly lift my spirits. Theo's precise words were, "I'll go anywhere in the world as long as I'm with you."

So off we went to the seaside resort of Bracciano, near Rome. I was enamoured with the glossy pictures, and the fact that Rome was easily accessible meant there were options if we'd exhausted all that the little island and its neighbouring villages had to offer. Theo had left it entirely up to me, so I just ran with it.

The first dampener, however, was the villa we shared with another couple and a single man in his thirties, Adam. It was no way as large or as luxurious as the brochures suggested. And although we each had our own self-contained units, complete with en suite and kitchenette, sharing only the lounge, the walls may as well have been made of cardboard. I could hear Adam on his phone and talking back to the baseball game on TV. The elderly couple were quieter, though on occasions I heard one or the other of them snoring.

And then, it rained non-stop. Which ruled out strolling along the sunny beach – ambling aimlessly in the rain was not my idea of a holiday. Visiting museums, markets and cathedrals wasn't Theo's. So we were stuck mostly in our little unit, Theo sulking and hugging the TV remote and me lost in my reading material, and dreams of my own cosy bed in England – preferably without Theo in it.

However, what made it one of the longest weeks of my life was that there wasn't much to distract me; I couldn't find any inspiration for my painting and there was no one to comfort me as I wrestled with the shadows of my losses. I took lots of showers so it could explain the soreness in my eyes. And oh, how sore they were…

So no, thanks, I wasn't prepared to give up my plans for the last summer with Sunita in my care for a two-week Mediterranean or Caribbean cruise with Theo. The chances of me jumping overboard were more real than I wanted to entertain.

I did try to let him down gently though. However, he took it real hard – giving me the silent treatment for a while, then barking at me for no reason, and then leaving his socks and stuff littered everywhere. When I got tired of picking up after him and tiptoeing around him, I took him to task last weekend.

"I take it you don't want your birthday party then?"

"What makes you say that?"

"Well, you are still not speaking to me – barking and grunting don't count – you're still going around the place like a wounded bear."

"I really wanted the cruise."

"I know. You can still have it, just at a later date."

"Yes, but I wanted it for my 40th, and I wanted you for myself."

"So, should I cancel the party then?" It was all I could do to keep my voice from breaking. I was now willing to concede – we could go on the cruise, I'd grin and bear it, I'd arrange something with Daisy so as to have times with Sunita in the school holidays (she wants to be doing the school runs so that she can be actively engaged in her life, she said to me). So yes, if that would get Theo out of the pits, then perhaps that was better than forcing him to be happy at his own birthday party. I guess the thought of coming back home to being available for Sunita would keep me sane as we sailed.

"Okay. I know it's a bit late in the day, but who knows, we might even get a last-minute deal and save ourselves a few pounds." By now, the enthusiasm was in the process of transforming from forced to real.

"No, Beauty," Theo said. Did I detect tenderness in his voice? "Let's leave it this time. We can have a cruise some other time, maybe to mark an anniversary – or even your birthday. Let's get on with the party – it sounds like so much fun."

That thoughtfulness really made me feel good on the inside. And the party was successful – at least largely. I'm not sure what to make of his little dig just before the games, but I plan to revisit that later. The guests were a thrill, really getting into it… and kindly complimenting the food, and everything really. My mind was going over all of this as I did the dishes when I heard what sounded like a row between Mel and Theo.

After she'd left, I went back to continue, needing to get everything out of the way, seeing to it that the house was childproof again and then to have a good night's rest before Sunita's arrival at 8am in the morning. When Theo padded along to drop his glass in the sink, I asked him, "So what was that about?"

He looked dazed. Staggered a bit. "Have you been drinking?"

"Not any more than my usual. I've just been thinking."

"What about?"

"About Melody and what she said."

The back of my neck tingled, and my tongue went dry. Eventually I managed, "So, are you going to tell me what she said?"

"I don't know that I should. She said she'll tell you herself."

Now my heart was racing. "Did anyone die?"

He chuckled, "No, Beauty, no one's died. But somebody was born."

"Please don't speak in riddles. Actually, why don't I just get the phone and call Mel myself?" He took one stride and was next to me by the sink. "No, don't call her. I'll tell you…" and muttered something under his breath.

Now my grip on the sink was so tight you could see my veins. He was pacing, his veins popping along his neck and temples. Eventually, he took in a deep breath.

"Beauty, it is both good news and bad news, all at once."

"Yes?"

"Ash is my baby."

"What?"

"Sweetie, Mel said that I am Ashleigh's father."

I was thinking that if this was a joke, it surely was in bad taste. "Is this even possible?" I tried to sound light.

His answer, however, was a subdued "Yes," with his eyes on his toes.

"You slept with Melody?"

"That was before us, sweetie – and obviously she

didn't tell you either. Some sister she is."

I was thinking 'I must still be asleep. I am not hearing what I think I am hearing. I want to wake up'.

"You had an affair with Melody?"

"I'm sorry. I did. But I chose you in the end, surely that must count for something?"

I was scratching myself for I'd begun to itch all over… it was all I could do to get my thoughts in order.

"And you never thought to tell me this before now?"

"I'm sorry, okay…"

"And so should you be, you lying conniving back-stabbing bastard!"

With each word, I'd flung an item at him. He ran round the kitchen playing 'dodge crockery', and then I went after him with two of the largest white dishes scream-ing, "Get out, get out of my life, now, get out…"

"Beauty, I'm sorry, we can work this out."

The more he said that, the angrier – and louder – I got. Then he stopped running and turned to face me. "Now put those dishes down or else…"

"Or else what? You'll call the police? You are the po-lice, so arrest me, you bastard."

"Beauty! Stop it!"

Now he was holding my arms. I was screaming, "Leave me alone," as I wriggled, trying – and failing – to free myself from his grip.

He was shaking me. "Stop it! Stop it, let's talk this through."

He was shaking me. Vigorously. Whipping my head back and forth; he kept shaking me, even as my screams gradually petered into a whimper… and then I went limp in his hands…

The next thing I knew, I felt myself up on the chandelier looking down at my form on the floor with my weeping husband banging the tiles with his fists and calling out my name again and again… and again…

CHAPTER 14

July 2006. Beauty's Funeral
Ashleigh (aged 16)

It was so good to ride with Josh back home after Uncle Theo's party. After all that he put me through at St Katherine's High, I didn't think I'd miss him that much when he left school. But not only had he left school, he'd left home. And it looks like going to college at Hull had done him a lot of good.

He was always good with his hands so I wasn't surprised when he told me he is getting jobs already although he had yet to complete his *Domestic Engineering* qualification. The only thing we argued over was his hair.

"When did you decide to go afro?"

"I didn't," he smiled. He is still irritating in giving me incomplete incomprehensible answers.

"Excuse me, what have you got on your head?"

"A head of hair."

"It's not low cut?"

"No."

"It's not plaits?"

"No."

"What is it then?"

"Just hair. Big hairdo." I could see the twinkle in his eyes when he glanced at me.

"But for the fact that you are trying to park this car in this tiny space, I'd have pulled your hair to find out for myself if it was indeed a head of hair."

As my curiosity was yet to be satisfied, I picked the subject up again after we had made ourselves drinks to wind down for the night.

"What's the story with the plaits anyway – and please, no more teasing."

"I still wear them. I believe they are an important part of my identity. So far they have neither interfered with my coursework nor jobs, so I'm good."

"But why are you out of them tonight?"

"It's Uncle Theo's birthday do, I know how he's like with stuff like that so I just wanted to chill out on that count."

"Now that was so thoughtful. I probably would have done the same, but only because I'm a little bit scared of him."

"Yeah, Uncle Theo can be scary sometimes, but he's good, I really admire him."

"I'm surprised to hear that. I thought you didn't care much for him?"

"I didn't. But looking back, I think he was gutsy to have taken the unpopular step of ensuring I was held accountable for my actions, even if it meant being in a cell for one night. And it's since then that I began to consider an alternative route to the journey of my life. What I saw… never mind."

"Go on Josh, you can tell me."

I saw the faint shadow flit across his face, which seemed to harden just a tiny bit, and then softened almost as quickly. Somehow that reminded me of Mum.

"That will be a story for another day."

So we just hung out, flicking through TV channels and talking about old friends. We were in the middle of a bellyful of laughter when Mum walked in, looking completely freaked.

"Hey, I didn't realise you'd both still be awake."

"You know us," Josh said, "we like to burn the midnight oil. What's the matter anyway? You look like you ran into *The Thriller*."

When she said nothing and went into the kitchen, I thought she was just tired and not in the mood for Josh's jokes. But she came back with a glass of something that was neither water nor fruit juice. As I didn't see where she poured it from I couldn't tell what exactly it was. It smelt potent. I was surprised she still had that kind of stuff stashed somewhere in the house. Anyway, she came back, sat at the dining table, looking at the stuff in her glass, and said, "I may actually have been in an episode of *The Thriller*."

"Mum, what happened?" I queried.

"Did somebody harass you?" Josh asked.

"There is something that I got off my chest today. Keeping it in all these years has nearly killed me with guilt. I don't know that I've done the right thing in letting it out. But now that I've started, I might as well go through with it."

My throat went so dry I couldn't say anything. I saw Josh open his mouth and close it again, anxiety written all over his face. Mum was silent like forever. When she spoke, her voice was like a combination of a tired old lady's and a frightened little girl's.

"I did something terrible many years ago. And for that I am sorry."

Me, I was still speechless with fear. This cannot be good. Josh finally spoke up, "Mum, if you want to tell us, do so; if not, then please just leave it. This suspense is unhealthy."

"I'm sorry. I'm so very sorry."

"And what is it you are sorry about?" I could hear the agitation in Josh's voice and now I was afraid of a confrontation between them.

"I lied by omission. And it has severe consequences." She was wringing her hands, and twisting in her seat. This couldn't be Mum. What could she have done?

"Josh, you know the truth about your dad, Nick."

"Yes, and what about him?"

"Nothing new, that was by way of introduction. Ash, Nick isn't your dad."

"Okay. I don't even know the guy and it doesn't really matter who is as whoever it was didn't bother to stick around, so big deal," I shrugged.

"Maybe if I'd told him I was expecting you, he may have decided differently."

"Do I really need to know all of this tonight? I've been fine all these years without a dad even though I thought Nick was him, but now he isn't. Okay, now I know why I'm severely messed up. Can we get on with it now? I have school tomorrow, remember?"

"I'm sorry, Ash, my baby. The truth is out, and it's best you hear the whole of it from me."

"If that will help you sleep well tonight, then out with it. If Nick isn't my dad, who is?"

"Theo."

It came out so quietly I was sure I'd misheard. "Sorry, who?"

"Theo." She was louder this time. "Your Uncle Theo is actually your dad."

"Do you know how messed up this sounds?"

"I do, and I am very sorry."

I began to feel a coldness travel through my whole body. And then a choking sensation, clammy hands, dry mouth. I knew it would turn out bad if I remained in the same room as my mum for much longer. Yet I couldn't say a word. Josh, bless him, took me by the hand and said, "We're going for a drive."

We drove around in silence for a while. I really couldn't speak. I answered Josh's questions with nodding, headshaking and monosyllables. But he got the message that going back home wasn't an option... so we ended up at Aunty Daisy and Uncle Rob's.

This was where we were when later the next day we received news about Aunty Beauty. How am I supposed to live with the truth that the man I thought was my dad wasn't and that my real dad is the uncle I feared who was married to the aunt I loved who was now dead? How am I supposed to live with the fact that my mum is a liar and that she might have something to do with Aunty Beauty's death, in which case she's a murderer also?

The funeral was delayed because the police wanted to keep the body for a while to do some more tests. As I am a kid and not direct next of kin, the officials don't tell me anything. And of course the adults in my life don't want to tell me anything so that they can keep lying to me. Josh is right. Taking a year out before I take my A levels and travelling the world will probably benefit me at this point in time. The earlier I get that waitressing job, the quicker I can get some experience under my belt.

Anyway, here we are at Aunty Beauty's funeral. Sometimes I think I see her out of the corner of my eye, she looks much more beautiful than when she was here with us. I wasn't going to come for the funeral. I couldn't bear the thought of being in the same room with my mother (who has to be here as she was her sister) and Uncle Theo (who has to be here as he was her husband). These were her next of kin. And they betrayed her. How long has this been going on, I wonder? And she died the night the truth came out? How very convenient.

In the run-up to today when I think I see her, often she looked like she was pleading. From when I decided I would attend her funeral purely to say my goodbyes, whenever I felt her, it was as though she were smiling. I don't believe in ghosts or anything but I've found it strangely comforting.

So, here we are at St Katherine's Church. Where I was christened. I think Aunty Beauty is here now, even as she was then. It's getting to Josh's and my turn in the Order of Service. I know what I want to say. But there are so many people out there, like proper adults, not children in a school assembly. And this is my Aunty Beauty's funeral service, I cannot afford to mess it up for her. If that thought were a painting, I'd have said the ink wasn't yet dry on it when I see Aunty Beauty's face right before me, sombre but not sad. Her grey-green eyes were as clear as a lake in the spring. Her nod was almost imperceptible. When I smiled, she smiled right back! If it were something else, someone else, I'd have thought I was going crazy. But this was my Aunty Beauty, my godmother and my friend.

As soon as I settled it once and for all that I would be speaking directly to Aunty Beauty, I was able to be still enough to hear the tail end of Josh's tribute:

"… and she didn't mind me plaiting my hair – she

would even plait it herself sometimes when Uncle Theo wasn't there. So I'm in plaits today to honour her, a free spirit who wanted everyone to live in liberty; who believed in responsibility and personal integrity..."

I've now stopped trying to wipe away my tears. What's the point? It's a funeral after all.

"... the kindest soul, gentle yet strong. To have been taken in the prime of her life, it is so unfair... yet she would want us to carry on with ours, to live it to the fullest and in truth. I cannot speak for anyone but myself. And so I say to you, Aunty Beauty, you may be gone from us today, but you live forever in my heart. And I will carry the banner of the things for which you stood – and for which you ultimately died..."

Is there something Josh knows that he is not telling me?

"... I will live my life to the fullest, in liberty and in truth, in honour of you..."

"And so will I," I hear myself whisper, "so will I."

July 2006. Beauty's Funeral
Melody

I cannot follow the service. From the moment Beauty's body was brought in to the singing of *Just as I am*, I've been shaking. It's just as well there's an Order of Service with all the songs, prayers and Josh's tribute in it because I'm simply not following. And I'm meant to be singing at some point, how am I going to get through with that? How and why did I even agree to it?

This should have been my funeral. Mine, me, Mel – the treacherous sister, the lying mother, the tactless fool.

If I'd kept my mouth shut all these years, why didn't I just keep on doing so? Now that I've satisfied that pang of conscience, where does that leave me? With sister dead. And children not speaking to me – to them, I'm as good as dead. And that is only fair. I can't fault anybody but myself.

Oh, it could have had such a different ending. How many times will I have to revisit that party?

There was the food and drinks to match the nautical theme and décor. Did I compliment her on those? If I did, it wasn't nearly enough. I so took her for granted. There was the musical statues. I thought that was better for grown-ups than musical chairs. Did I tell her that? I doubt it. Then the beach bingos. That was a new one on me to be frank, but I enjoyed it. And yes, my team won the Pictionary contest. How could such a lovely evening have gone so wrong? Because I couldn't keep my big mouth shut, that's why.

And then there was the cake cutting, and cheering and eating and drinking. And then it gradually drew to a close.

Everyone left for home. If only I'd gone with them, things would have ended up differently. But even though I'd stayed, things could still have ended up differently. For example, I could have stayed to help clear up, but asked Ash and Josh to stay and help too – after all, they are family. And then the conversation would not have happened.

Or I stayed to help, but gravitated to Beauty in the kitchen, and chatted with her instead, after all, she is – was – my sister.

Or I stayed to help, got into a conversation with Theo, and cut it short before the great confession. What a fool, a big tactless fool I've been.

They obviously fought after I'd gone. Theo wouldn't tell me over what. But his fingerprints were indelible on her arms. He said all he did was restrain her as she attacked him. Beauty wouldn't say boo to a goose, let alone attack anyone. What did he say to her to cause her to react in that way?

Theo's voice brings me back. "I am reading from the book of Revelation, chapter 21, verses 1 to 5." I'm surprised to hear the steadiness in his voice, powerful as always. It was only after the pause was longer than usual that I realised he also was struggling to keep his emotions in check.

I remember the first time I set eyes on him. He towered above the crowd at Notting Hill Gate. We were all eager to get on the next train, whether space permitted it or not. Beauty and I were behind him on the platform, but he made sure we got in before he did. It turned out we were all headed in the same direction of East London. My other attraction to him was how knowledgeable he was. He'd recently graduated from the University of East London, and was contemplating an MBA. His dad was a prominent politician in Nigeria who feared for his own life and that of his only son as he'd received threats from the ruling military dictatorship. He was a bit undecided whether his stay would be temporary. He was restless. Until he married Beauty and decided to make East London his home. (Or thinking about it now, did he decide to make East London his home and therefore married Beauty?)

I can't help wondering what he would do now. What we had was a reckless fling. I was on the rebound from Nick. Theo seemed attentive at first but then withdrew. I didn't explore it further as I was hoping to patch it up with Nick anyway. When eventually Beauty told me they were going together, I thought about telling her then, but decided against it. I felt she deserved a good man in her life, and from what I could see at the time, Theo was it for her. I didn't want to spoil it with 'too much information'.

It wasn't until later that I realised I was pregnant. I've never stopped wondering what his reaction would have been if I'd told him I was expecting Ashleigh.

And Beauty, should I have told her? I guess I know the answer to that now. Would she have believed me? Would she have understood? Would she have forgiven me, eventually? I will never know that now. But she probably, most likely, would still have been alive. Hating me, yes, but still alive.

I'm beginning to see that I'm responsible for Beauty's death. Theo said he had to stop her from attacking him. If she attacked him, then he said something to set her off. And if he told her that I said he was Ashleigh's father, then that would have been the trigger. And since I gave him the information, I was responsible for the chain that eventually crushed her. After this is all done and dusted, I will hand myself in. I have nothing else to lose. Although I didn't pull the trigger, I most certainly loaded the gun, and I should pay for that.

I was amazed at the sense of peace I felt when I made that resolution. Apparently Theo had finished his reading, I'd missed several steps in the Order of Service including the address, and the slot for quiet personal reflection was drawing to an end. Rev Craig now calls on Ashleigh to say a few words.

I'll have to make myself focus long enough to hear everything she has to say as Ash didn't give in her tribute in time to make it into the printed Order of Service. But it's hard as seeing Ash's slight frame in a black halter-neck dress with a silver and black bolero walk up to the lectern, all at once I could see Beauty as a teen, giving a valedictory speech at the end of her A levels...

"... *Aunty Beauty saved my life in many ways*" (but it was Ash who was speaking) "... *she was the mother that I never really had... and her husband was the father I never knew about until a fortnight ago.*" (The gasp from the congregation was palpable) "... *I bet she didn't know that until that night either. And somehow, I don't know, but I kind of feel that that knowledge has something to do with her untimely death... but I'm only a kid, nobody tells me anything that matters, when it really matters.*" (She shot her eyes in my direction. Oh if looks could kill, I'd have been happy to have died just then. As she went on, I could feel the fire raging in her belly, and I know I am to blame for all that anger, all that hate... and I am the one who really deserves to be in the casket, or at best, in jail.)

"*Yes, I'm just a kid who knows nothing. And nobody, I repeat nobody tells me anything that matters, when it really matters. Apart from my Aunty Beauty. Now she's gone. Has she really gone? Is this a dream, a nightmare of sorts? Is somebody going to wake me up sometime soon? Is this a joke?*" (I'm willing myself to listen... there's so much sniffling and whispering going on, I am really straining to hear... and not to weep.)

"*I'm sorry I don't really have much to say... I really couldn't think of any one thing to say hence I didn't script my speech today... I do think there are questions to be asked. But who cares enough to ask them? The ones who betrayed her? The ones who ignored her? Or the ones who nobody will listen to, because of their age?*

I will therefore speak to my Aunty Beauty: I do hope you are in a better place, that you are happy, and that you are at peace. Because if anyone deserves to be happy at all, that person most certainly is you.

Thank you for sharing your life with me, your love of words and your joy in painting. I will never forget you as long as I live, you and your funny quirky ways. And I hope that one day…" (she chokes, and pauses) *"… that one day…"* (a deep sigh) *"… that one day I will see you again, and we'll be together forever…"* (she looks to Josh, who is promptly by her side, leading her away from the lectern)…

As Rev Craig intones, "Let us pray," we all rise. After this item, it's my turn to sing my farewell to Beauty, and then a final hymn by the congregation before we proceed to the cemetery.

It had been extremely difficult having to choose an appropriate song for such an inappropriate issue as an unexpected premature death of my one and only sister. And I'm not sure where Beauty is headed (I'm not sure where I'm headed after my death for that matter) but I had to be hopeful. I had no other choice. Hence *There's a Place Where the Streets Shine*, the following lyrics being key:

> *No more pain, no more sadness,*
> *No more suffering, no more tears.*
> *No more sin, no more sickness,*
> *No injustice, no more death . . .*

How I'm going to actually carry it through is another matter entirely…

July 2006. Beauty's Funeral
Theo

I'm sure this is why she was called Melody… what a powerful rendition… she speaks for all of us in that song…

What a mess I've made of everything. Absolutely everything… Mel is right. Beauty, I hope, is now in a place where she will be free from every kind of pain, including those inflicted unintentionally which don't hurt any less nonetheless.

Beauty's death has thrown up issues for me at both personal and professional levels. It's just as well that my testimony was accepted – I was restraining her as she attacked me. And that is rightly what happened. That is the fact.

The truth of the matter though is that there were other options.

Option number one: I could have just stood there and taken her beatings and beratings. I could easily have deflected the crockery. She was angry. She had every right to be. She was in shock and was acting contrary to her character. I should have known that. If I'd just stood there and taken it like a man, she'd have eventually run out of steam, and we could then have had a conversation. The only thing that would have been dented would have been my pride.

Option number two: I could have walked away. She probably would have followed me, but not if I'd run to the car and driven off. I know I can outrun her, I've proved it on so many occasions: if I wanted to show I was very upset, I'd sprint to the car and screech off. It irritated her. But I did it anyway. This would have been a good time to have done that, given her time to cool off before picking up the conversation. If I'd done that, the only person who would have suffered would have been my ego. Beauty would most probably still be alive.

Option three: I could have held my peace and let Mel break it to her when she'd planned it all out. She obviously knew that Beauty would take it badly hence she said to leave it to her. I should have just have sat back and allowed the sisters to sort it out between themselves.

Option four: If I were talking to somebody else, I'd have said they could have restrained her by holding her hands behind her back. I could have done that. Effortlessly. Would have done that if somebody were being unreasonable in the streets and was resisting arrest. Why didn't I do that? Honestly, it was because I was angry. More like enraged. I didn't really have to shake her to stop her.

But I did. I did shake her. Far too much. Far too hard. She did slip away rather quickly though… I have wondered whether she had any undiagnosed conditions. She didn't seem to have put up a fight for her life… I don't know… all I do know is that I shouldn't have shaken her. And somehow I can't seem to get past that.

The service is coming to an end now. I'm one of the pall-bearers, naturally, as is Josh – who doesn't look me in the eye. Neither does Ash. And Mel, I can almost touch the anger oozing at me when I've had to speak with her. Yet she can't blame me a hundred per cent. Or can she?

What am I supposed to do now? From being married and childless to being widowed and a father to a teenage girl. What shall I do about Ash? Is it even true? How can I know for sure, without subjecting anyone to tests and further anguish? Beauty was good with things like that. She'd have helped me navigate the waters after she'd calmed down. I should have known better. If only it hadn't been Mel. Beauty was so angry – I'd never seen her that angry. Yet she's right. I should have told her about me and Mel. I should have understood her anger. I should have stood by and taken it till it subsided – and it would have… why didn't I just do that?

"Dust to dust… ashes to ashes," Rev Craig brings me back as he speaks the closing blessings.

The journey to her final resting place was so quiet I could almost hear the grey matter groaning in my brain. For most of it, it was like I was in a trance. I noticed a few bowed heads as the hearse drove along London Road to the cemetery, but that was about it. Near full automaton seemed to have set in.

Bearing the casket. Lowering it into the grave. Throwing in the last rose and the first shovel of earth. Saying goodbye to Beauty has been the most painful experience in my life. We were supposed to be together till ripe old age. We were going to go on that cruise, we were going to have babies, even if eventually we had to adopt, we were going to work it all out… and we could have worked this out… if only I hadn't shaken her so hard…

I'm not ready to leave her just yet. I just can't… I'll meet the others at the reception in a little while. For now, I sit on the nearest bench to Beauty's grave, resolutely focusing on options for a tombstone for one as loving, innocent and kind as she was. All my glazed eyes can see, however, is an empty weedy lane ahead of me that stretches out as if to eternity…

EPILOGUE

July 2006. The Funeral
Beauty

At 10 o'clock this morning, the bells of St Katherine's Church chimed 35 times, one for every year of my life.

They all look so sad, so broken, so lost. My departure was sudden so they must still be in shock. For me, the shock was how much lighter I felt, and how much faster too. And free. I know I'm on my way to the place where the sun never sets, where there'll be no more pain, no more tears. But for now, I want to hang around and say my goodbyes – not that anyone can see or hear me, except for Ash who senses me sometimes. Still, I want to leave my well wishes behind, hoping that those will, in time, wipe away a tear or two.

Look at Sunita. I'm glad she isn't dressed in black. Her little white and yellow dress is a breath of fresh air in the sea of dark blues, greys and blacks. I whisper a 'thank you' to Daisy who seems to have shrunk; her eyes are sunken, and Rob, the rock who looks like he's crumbling.

And Josh – such a picture of dignity. His composure. His manner. His words about me, and to me. What a comfort! I'm glad he's looking out for Ash who is fiery on the outside and all eaten up on the inside. My dear Ash. For one so young to speak such truth with boldness and to have such insight. Between the pair of them, I worry that they might not let the incident be the unfortunate accident that it was. And ultimately what the implications might be for Theo.

It was an accident. I know Theo didn't mean it the way it turned out. I'm certainly more useful to him alive than dead (even though he often called me 'useless'). Yet, even while I was alive and well, what many didn't realise was that various parts of me were getting either atrophied or fragmented… I guess it is difficult to really see past what it is we want to see…

Seeing how shattered he is, I just want to get it across to him that I forgive him, for everything, that is everything… but of course he can't hear me…

And Mel, what was she thinking? Why didn't she tell me all these years? Now she's gone and lost everything. Grieving as she is on so many levels, she is still able to spread such comfort with her singing. Whether she's received any comfort herself is yet to be seen.

The graveside. After Theo, Josh and the other pall-bearers lower my casket into the ground, Sunita, cradled by Daisy, with Rob holding her hand, throws in the first single red rose. Then Ash throws in a white one, and Josh a red one. The next is a white one from Mel, a red from Daisy and a white from Rob followed by a red one from Theo. Between the five of them, they throw in 35 red and white roses in perfect synchronicity. How they managed to arrange that when half of them aren't yet speaking to one another, I don't know. It has to be Daisy's handiwork.

And then comes the time for the earth to be shovelled in. Theo takes the lead in this. And while the shovelling is going on, the grave sounds of mud against casket are muffled by Mel's beautiful encore of *There's a Place Where the Streets Shine.* I don't think that was planned. Many join in… I do as well, but nobody hears me…

As they file back to the car park, each lost in their

own thoughts, memories and grief, I hear Theo say to Rob that he needs to stay behind for a bit, and that he will join them in a little while. Rob carries on to the car park, but doesn't drive away. Daisy and Sunita ride home with Josh and Ash. The reception is taking place at theirs.

Theo sits himself on a bench. I sit next to him, placing my hand on his. He withdraws it almost immediately, rubbing it briskly, as if he were cold. He looks in my direction, but his eyes are gazing way past me, past the seas of headstones and tombs, past the trees, plants and hedges, far away into the horizon... I know, of course, that I'm invisible to him, as I always was. Only this time, I'm not invisible to myself also.

I cannot linger here any longer. My homecoming party is in full swing. My chief host is here to lead me there – to that place where I shall be known, and loved, and forever called Beautiful.

I turn to face him, and cannot suppress my gasp... I'm beginning to take delight in my reflection which I'm seeing in his eyes... for his smile is rapidly washing away the every imperfection of my face...

Notes/Glossary

1. *Chinchin* and *puff puff* are Nigerian snacks made of dough.

2. *Pounded yam* – a smooth dough of mashed yam, akin to mashed potatoes but of firmer consistency. Traditionally it's made by pounding boiled yam pieces with pestle and mortar. Nowadays though, it can be made in a pot using yam flour and hot water.

3. *Egusi soup* – a kind of soup thickened with melon seeds. It has many varieties to it, goes well with pounded yam amongst other accompaniments.

4. *Born throw-way* – derogatory, similar to bastard, implies one who doesn't know or has forsaken their roots.

5. *Oga* – master, boss, chief, governor.

6. *Molue* – big yellow buses in Lagos, the *molue* is distinctive for its ricketiness, the antics of the bus conductors and the fact that the bus hardly completely stops at the bus stop. It takes a peculiar skill to get on and get off it and remain standing on one's two feet. Overcrowding is the rule in *molues*, but it is the cheapest form of transportation in Lagos.

7. *Yam and Peppersoup* – Peppersoup is a light (texture) spicy soup that can be eaten as an appetiser or with yam or unripe plantains as a main meal.

8. *Up and down* – a two-piece wrapper made of special fabrics such as wax print, fancy print, tie-and-dye (adire) or George.

9. *George* – a more expensive fabric used for special occasions.

10. *Gele* – a traditional headpiece – different communities use different fabrics/textures, and they can go from simple to elaborate, depending on the occasion, and of course on personal preference.

11. *Itsekiri* and *Urhobo* are historical rival ethnic groups in the Warri area along with the *Ijaw.*

12. *Oyibo* – a white person in Warri pidgin. In other parts of Nigeria, it's *oyinbo.*

13. *Urhobo-wayo* – a play on the *Urhobo* greeting *Urhobo wado* and also a stereotypical description of the *Urhobo* people as being cunning.

14. *NEPA* – the Nigeria Electric Power Authority is responsible for supplying electric power. However, because of its inefficiency, it got corrupted to mean **Never Expect Power Always.** Whenever there's a power cut, there's a general outcry – NEPA!

15. *Jollof rice* – a popular Nigerian dish made with rice and a tomato-based sauce.

16. *Moimoi* – steamed beans pudding.

17. *Dodo* – ripe plantains sliced or diced and fried.

18. *Ashawo* – prostitute in pidgin.

19. *Ewuwu* – a type of mask/masquerade in some parts of Nigeria, typically terrifying.

About the Author

Rita Ese Edah is passionate about helping people overcome barriers. A mother of three, playing with the family pet dog and crocheting random pieces help her to unwind from the stresses of daily living.